Timber Beast
Twisted Tales of Familiar Faces
A.K. Hughey

M4L Publishing

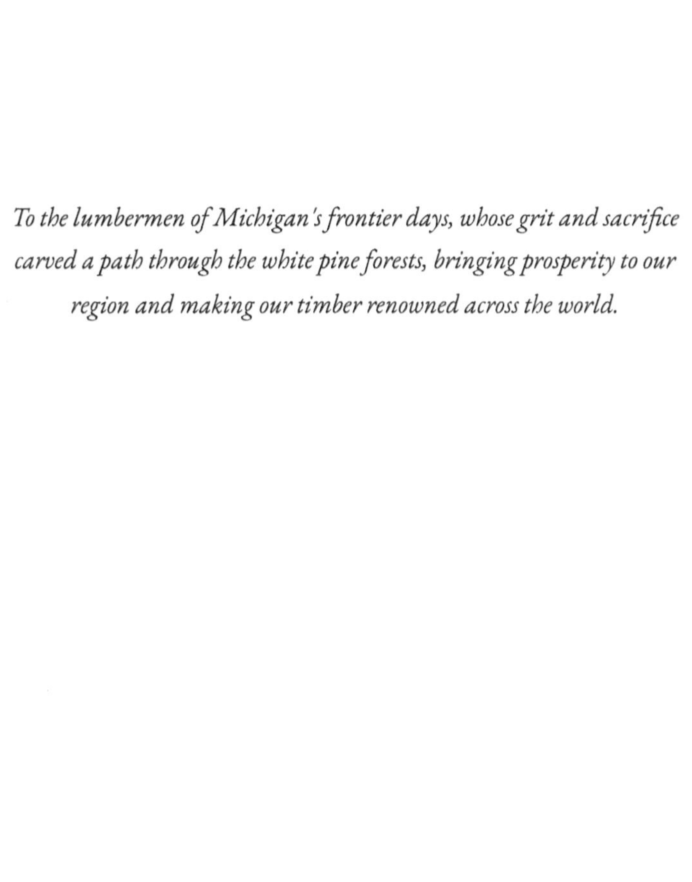

To the lumbermen of Michigan's frontier days, whose grit and sacrifice carved a path through the white pine forests, bringing prosperity to our region and making our timber renowned across the world.

Prologue – The Wrong Way

THE HEAD SHOULDN'T HAVE been turned around like that, or the neck crooked the way it was. Fabian stood frozen merely three strides away from the deer carcass and studied it. He couldn't explain the sick feeling growing in the pit of his stomach or why the hairs stood up on the back of his neck, but he was trying desperately to rationalize it anyway.

Although it was getting late and his sawyer partner Viggo had warned him not to walk out of sight of their supplies, Fabian had heard the deer bawling and couldn't stop himself from seeking out the injured animal. Viggo had walked away to relieve himself, and Fabian hated the sound of the animal crying in pain, so he had picked his way through the old growth until he found it. He was too late to help the creature.

A bear could have been capable of this kind of damage. But he'd grown up in the Canadian wilderness, and he never saw a bear-mauled carcass twisted around and torn up like this. The head had been wrenched to face the wrong way at the top of the neck, the torso turned the opposite way. Each of its four legs had been broken in multiple places, and the neck and stomach slashed open. Even the tail hadn't been spared—it lay limp against the middle of the spine, its blood-covered white ridges visible through the gore.

Fabian fought the churning sickness in his stomach. There was no smell of decay here, only blood, and that realization sent a cold chill through his veins.

All the innards were left on the ground, and the meat remained untouched. If a bear, wolf, or some other predator had hunted the deer, it would have at least started to eat its kill. This was... wasteful. And cruel. As if whatever had done this had enjoyed torturing the doe.

He gripped the handle of his ax tighter, rubbing his thumb along the smooth wood grain as he glanced around for tracks or scat.

And he prayed to God that whatever had mutilated the deer wasn't still around.

His throat parched, Fabian swallowed hard as he swatted away a buzzing fly that came to inspect him. The shadows were getting long as daylight fled the sky, and his partner would be looking for him soon. Slowly, he turned around to go back the way he'd come, ready to put the mangled carcass far behind him.

He froze mid-step, breath shuddering out of him as he took in the sight of the creature crouching in a tangle of underbrush and saplings. It was steeped in the shadows of the trees, but a few slices of daylight cut across its body to reveal mangy black fur, sharp teeth, and deer-like antlers jutting from the top of its head.

Fabian didn't need the final shreds of daylight to see its eyes; the damn things glowed red from the darkness as the creature stared straight at him. The beast let out a low growl that rumbled through the air and vibrated in Fabian's bones.

Muscles trembling, Fabian willed himself to raise his ax, to defend himself. He knew the thing meant to kill him like it had killed the doe.

Malevolence filled the air between them, carrying the scent of decay and rot to Fabian's nostrils.

"Drop to your belly!"

Fabian threw himself to the ground without question and covered his head as a gun fired. The creature roared in pain, and Fabian sensed something leap over him, then heard it thunder away.

"*Hvad fanden*!" Viggo shouted in his thick Danish accent as he grabbed Fabian by the arm and hauled him up. "I told you not to go out alone!"

"What... what was that?" Fabian asked, picking up his ax before sprinting back to camp with Viggo.

"That is one of the things we don't talk about. Don't you tell a soul what you saw today. You hear?"

From that day on, Fabian soaked in every word the seasoned jacks had to spare for him. And he kept quiet about the thing he saw in the woods, the monster that would have ripped him apart if Viggo hadn't saved him.

Hell's Half Mile

PAUL FOURNIER WRAPPED HIS fingers around Silver Jack's neck, squeezing for all he was worth. There wouldn't be any "logger's pox" for him today—or ever. Jack fought in vain to break the hold until he punched upward against Paul's elbows. The pain licked like lightning through Paul's arms, and he stumbled backward. Before he could recover, Jack grabbed him by the shirt and belt and hefted Paul's whole body up before slamming him hard onto the bar top. Glasses crashed to the wood floor, though the sound could hardly be heard above the roar of the surrounding crowd.

Some men—and even the pretty server girls—cheered for either Paul or Jack, but most were shouting above the sea of noise to place their bets on who would win and who would be branded with the boot-caulk stamp—the dreaded "logger's pox" —on their face today.

Jack delivered a wild punch into Paul's gut, and Paul barely kept himself together as he spun to plant his boot into Jack's stomach and kick the bigger man back. It was just the break he needed. Paul rolled off the bar and sprinted forward, headfirst. Everyone in the country knew him for his thick skull, the most famed of his weapons, even above his giant meaty fists.

An inch taller even than Paul and much broader around the shoulders, Jack was a giant of a man, and far more agile than anyone Paul had ever battled before. He dodged at the last minute, and it was too late for Paul to stop. With his full momentum and one hundred eighty pounds of body weight, he rammed one of the saloon's eight-by-eight support columns.

If he hadn't nearly knocked himself out, Paul might have felt the building shudder as those around him had. A few people ran out the front door, unnerved by the unintended assault on the structure.

Paul saw double now but shook himself until he saw straight enough to duck a haymaker coming for his face. He charged forward, tackling Jack around the waist, and heaved him bodily to the floor. In a flash, he straddled him and pummeled the man's already swelling face until Jack blocked the blows with his arms, making himself as small a target as he could.

Once more, Paul's fingers found their way to Jack's neck and squeezed. He grunted with the effort, pushing down with his body weight as he sought to cut off the sour man's air. At the moment, he didn't think about whether he actually wanted to harm this timber feller. They were essentially brothers of the woods, but had always worked in different camps.

A single wrong word and a shove had kicked off the brawl of the century, a brawl the locals would talk about for decades to come.

Paul couldn't think then; he only felt the urge to rid himself of the threat Jack posed to his own life. And, truthfully, his pride as well. Jack loved to leave his caulk mark on the men he defeated, and he'd promised the pox to Paul.

Jack punched weakly at Paul's face, but Paul stretched his head away, out of reach of Jack's full force. Just as the light seemed to leave Jack's eyes, he delivered a desperate blow to the middle of Paul's chest, right at the bottom of his ribs. The wind whooshed from Paul's lungs, and he fell backward with the force of the blow. He ached for breath, even as the crowd roared, booed, and laughed around him. Their faces blurred, their voices becoming an indistinguishable mass of ugly noise.

He pushed up to his knees, desperate to suck in a breath, and spotted Jack on his side, his body racking with coughs. Paul tried to rise but stumbled, dizzy and still out of breath. The adrenaline was wearing off, and the aches were setting in. His knuckles and his head throbbed. Even his long legs protested his full weight on them. But he pushed himself forward again, rising to his full six-foot and three inches and starting toward Silver Jack again.

Jack, still coughing in between heaving, ragged breaths, shook his head and held up a weak hand. "No more," he rasped.

His thick Irish accent was barely distinguishable from the strain in his voice.

"You swear that." Paul ground out the words, more of a statement than a question.

"I swear it," the Irishman promised. He swallowed gingerly and rubbed his throat as he sat up, leaning back against the wooden support Paul had nearly taken out.

A waitress in a fine dress placed a delicate hand on Paul's elbow and smiled as she gestured toward the bar. "I'll bring you somethin' for your cuts."

Ruby always saw to him while he was there at the Red Bird Saloon, and on fighting nights, she'd give her attention to no one else. He liked to think it was because she was fond of him, but he knew her boss demanded that she take care of men like him: fighters and money-spenders.

Around them, people clapped or whistled, commending Paul on his win until he shot them all a swollen glare. Their cheers died to a murmur as Paul turned, slow and careful not to stumble, and leaned against the bar before wiping the blood from his nose and mouth.

The energy of the crowd deflated. In Hell's Half Mile, they were blood-hungry, especially for men with fighting reputations like Paul and Jack. He knew they'd wanted more. They'd wanted to see death that night. The law never came 'round here, 'specially not for the lumberjacks, most of whom were immigrants from Canada and northern Europe, escaped or freedmen from the South, natives, and the Métis or those of mixed race. Those who died in these wild lands, the frontiers of so-called civilization, disappeared without a trace.

"A brandy," Silver Jack ordered, taking the spot next to Paul along the bar, then gestured at him. "And another for my friend here."

"*Merci.*" Paul took the shot in one gulp, wincing at the various stings in and around his mouth as the liquor hit his cuts. Just then, Ruby came back with a bowl of water and a cloth. She hesitated, but after he nodded, she tended to his wounds. It stung, but he flinched less in front of her. She'd always been kind and gentle, keeping an eye on him whenever he had drunk too much, regardless of whether he'd riled up betting with his fists.

"Never met a man who could go toe to toe with me." Jack gulped down his drink, hissed at the pain, and ordered another round. "I'm Jack. And who are you, big man?"

"Fabian Fournier, but these," and he gestured lazily at the room behind them with one hand, "they call me Paul BonJean."

"You from France then? Or Canada?"

"Quebec."

"Remind me to stay out of Quebec if they're all built like you."

The waitress rounded the bar and poured fresh water in another bowl before returning to her ministrations.

"Well, I'm gonna find me a bath and a bed. I'll see you around, Paul BonJean."

Paul didn't turn, simply waved one bloody-knuckled hand at Jack.

By the time Jack was out the door, Ruby had finished with Paul's face and started on his knuckles. "Are you all right?"

"*Oui*," Paul lied. He hurt all over, as if a team of horses had stampeded over him, followed by a team of oxen.

"We could go somewhere quiet," she suggested. "Somewhere more private, so I can take care of you."

He turned his head slowly to stare into her pretty blue eyes. "My money is almost gone, Ruby. I cannot pay you."

Instead of cursing him or slapping him as the others would have, she only nodded and continued cleaning the blood from his hands. "I'll be here if you change your mind."

Unable to stop himself, he grinned through the pain. Stiffness had already begun settling in his limbs, and he knew he had to get back to the hostel and lie in his bunk before it got much worse. It was two blocks of walking to get back there, all while hiding his limp to keep from getting attacked by any late-night opportunists.

"How much?" He nodded toward the empty shot glasses.

"Nothin'," she whispered, winking at him. "All that bettin' these boys did? The winners will spend their dollars here."

"I must go," he said, rising, but she gripped his arm.

"Wait. I... I have something to ask of you."

"I already told you, Ruby. I cannot pay—"

"No, no. It's not that. It's... It's my nephew, Thomas. My sister's child. I've cared for him ever since she died. His pa and all the rest of our family is gone, but he's nine now, and it's getting harder to keep him out of trouble in this part of town."

Paul studied her glittering eyes, and for the first time since he'd known her, spotted a fear he'd never seen in her.

"I'm trying to save up and get us outta here, but Mr. Smith don't wanna let me out of this life. And now he's sayin' he wants the boy to earn his way here too."

He couldn't help it. Paul shook his head violently. He must have misheard her. "What? How do you mean?"

"Well... I- I can't say, exactly. But it's not good. I can't let that happen to him."

"This is very hard to hear, Ruby. Tell me what you wish to ask of me, *s'il vous plaît.*"

"I know you're scouting, that you're the land-looker for Langley Lumber this season."

"One of a few. They own so much. *Mais oui,* I am a land-looker this season."

"So, that means you'll be taking your crew out to survey the winter's cuttings in a few weeks, right?"

"Oui! What are you asking?" He spoke too loudly, and a few faces in the crowd glanced their way.

"Shhh!" she urged, resting a hand on his shoulder.

Tears brimmed in her eyes, threatening to fall, and a fire started deep in Paul's chest. He wanted to rip the hands and heads off of every man in the room, and have a long, slow talk with Matthew Smith.

"Please, Paul, keep your voice down, and don't tell anyone what we've talked about." She sniffled and blinked back the tears before continuing. "He's all I have left of my sister. I loved her, and I love that boy. But I think he'd be safer out there in the woods with you than here with me, at least until I can make enough money to get the hell outta here. I..." She let her words falter and her gaze fall. "I'm so tired, Paul."

She leaned her head against his shoulder and stroked her fingers along his back. He wasn't a fool; he knew she was putting on a show in case her boss, any of his goons, or jealous customers might be watching them.

Paul wouldn't let his emotions show. He grit his teeth as his heart broke for her. Clenching his fists, he held them glued to the bar top lest they raged through the room against his will. If he could have his way, he'd kill every low-down man in the saloon and carry Ruby out of there like the princess she was. And he'd bring the boy too.

Memories flickered through his mind in bits and pieces. Children huddled around a small fireplace in the dead of winter. Tales of ladies, knights, and chivalry that his father had read to Paul and his siblings from Sir Thomas Malory's *Le Morte d'Arthur*.

La Chevalerie demanded that Paul assist the lady, now begging for his help.

"Can the boy cook? If he can help in the cook shack, I will not only take him, I will give him a job. He will be paid well enough for a cookee, and it should help you get out of Hell's Half Mile that much sooner."

"Oh, Paul!" Her eyes glittered with tears again, but this time there was a flash of hope behind them.

His sense of pride swelled ten times more at giving her hope and safe refuge than it had when Silver Jack had finally given up the fight.

"I will send word for when and where he should meet us. I will buy everything he needs." Paul drew one thick finger gently down her perfect cheek, then lifted her chin and smiled as he stared down into her eyes. "Dry your tears, mademoiselle. It will be all right. *Au Revoir*."

Then he lifted himself from the bar stool again, this time patting Ruby's hand when she protested, and walked out of the saloon with his dignity intact.

A cool breeze caressed the tender flesh of his throbbing face as he stepped out into the midnight air. It was a meager reward for winning tonight's battle royale. He had withstood the blows of the meanest man in Saginaw Country, and saved his face. Though his face was now cut, bruised, and battered, at least there wasn't any "pox." He sighed as he considered what hardships a man had to endure to survive even the "civilized" parts of the north country.

This Is Not a Negotiation

Two weeks later, Paul stepped onto the porch of the Langley Lumber Company's Bay City office and took his hat off before stepping through the door. Inside the wide room, Paul spotted the familiar parlor area to his left, the counters to the right where men could come to apply for work or collect their pay, and the staircase in the middle of the room which led up to the second floor. The boss's office was up there, along with a handful of other rooms to which he'd never been invited.

The lone man in the room leaned over the counter, resting his chin on one hand. In his other hand, he held an open dime novel, the popular *Malaeska*. His gaze flicked upward to study Paul, but upon recognition, he tipped his head toward the stairs and returned his attention to the book.

"Well, good morning to you too," Paul muttered as he strode across the open room and then headed up the stairs.

"Paul, good to see you, son," his boss, Frederick, said, greeting him at the door to his office. "Come, sit with me. Will you have coffee this morning?"

"Yes, please." Paul schooled his language in the presence of the company man, aware that the Anglo-Saxon descendants preferred English and looked down on those who couldn't learn and apply it quickly.

They shook hands, then Paul sat, accepted a steaming cup of black liquid, and sipped while he listened to his boss.

"I'm glad to see you're still excited about the survey expedition," Frederick said, holding eye contact.

"Yes. I am grateful to have been chosen as a land-looker this year."

Fred nodded. "No... concerns?"

"And what concerns should I have?"

The boss shook his head, smiled so broadly he bared nearly all his teeth, and leaned back in his plush, velvet-lined chair. "None. Of course."

An eerie silence hung between them, and Paul couldn't deny the still, heavy air and the mystery lingering in the room with them. "Is there something I should know?"

Fred took another sip of coffee before answering. "I see you're still healing from your row with Silver Jack."

Paul shifted uncomfortably in his chair. "I am healed. This," he gestured to the fading cuts and bruises on his face, "is unfortunate. But it does not keep me from my duties."

"The entire town has been jabbering ever since it happened. They won't shut up about it. Hell, I think they're even talking about the 'bar fight of the century' down in Detroit." Fred dropped his cup on his desk with a thud, the black liquid spilling out and marring the perfect, clean wooden top. He stood, turned his back on Paul, and stared out the window and down toward the main thoroughfare.

Paul wanted to say something, but he didn't know what. He'd already reassured the boss that he'd be fine to work and complete the expedition. What else could be so important?

"They're saying that a BonJean, known as Saginaw Paul, is a mean cuss working for Langley Lumber. They're asking why Langley needs to hire such brutes."

"All the jacks are rough, but they are civilized, no?"

Fred nodded. "But they don't get reputations that cross the state—and maybe farther—like you do. It's not a good look for the company, Paul."

"My bruises?"

"No, your drinking, fighting, and carousing as soon as you get back to town." He turned back to Paul, hands on his hips. "Now I know all the jacks like to do it, but most of them aren't as memorable as you, with your height, a-and your—" He pointed to his mouth, likely referencing Paul's unusual teeth. Instead of finishing his scolding rant, he scoffed and returned his gaze to the thoroughfare.

"I was only defending myself, monsieur." He flinched internally when he realized he'd spoken the last word in French. Fred always seemed annoyed by the language.

Fred didn't acknowledge the claim.

"I will be gone for one or two months, and there will be no fighting. See? It is okay."

"You know, Paul," Fred started, shaking a finger toward the street before turning to glare daggers at Paul. "I could pick any man off that street right now to do the job for half of what I'm paying you."

Paul's stomach dropped. He'd been looking forward to this, striving for it ever since his second season. And he'd already quit his carpentry job. Sure, old Bill might take him back, but he didn't want to change his plans, to return in shame with his tail between his legs.

"What do you need me to do, sir?"

"I need you to promise me, no more rows! No more fighting, not with Silver Jack, and not with anybody else. I want you to stay out of Hell's Half Mile. The minute you take one step back in that den of sin, I'll hear about it, and you'll be blacklisted from Langley and every other lumber company in the north country. Hell, I'd suspect you'd have to go all the way to California or Alaska to find a job in lumber again. But my partner and brother leads our sister company out on the West Coast, so you'd be out of luck there too."

"I don't understand. I am a good customer—"

"This is not a negotiation. You either agree to stay out of that side of town, or you give up lumberin', including the expedition that's supposed to launch in just two hours."

Paul was still confused, but he didn't see that he had any choice. This was his livelihood, work he enjoyed, and probably the only thing he'd ever be good at. He nodded solemnly. "I swear I will stay out of Hell's Half Mile, boss."

"My brother will be here in two weeks to meet with me and review the company's progress. Nothing, Paul, nothing can go wrong! So no more fighting, and no more drinking like you enjoy doing. The kind where you keep going until you can't see your own hands in front of your face."

Damn it. "No fighting, no drinking, boss. I... I understand."

"And... I have a man joining you for the expedition."

"Who?" Paul shifted in his seat as he ground his teeth. "Do I need a... chaperone?"

Fred didn't laugh. "Paul, a man like me running an operation like this needs to be sure of his investments. The man joining you has my full faith, and he represents my interests."

"So, who is he?"

"It's better if you meet him on the morning of your departure."

"Ugh. *Merde.*" Paul couldn't keep from grimacing. As if his first expedition as land-looker wasn't already turning out to be strange and stressful enough, his boss had added some unknown wildcard to the equation. "Fine, fine. You are the boss."

Fred's mood flipped from stern and as angry as a bull to relaxed and full of smiles. The rapidity of the change was unsettling. "Good. I've already prepared your saddlebags and two sets of maps. One set for you and one for Makwa."

"Merci," Paul said, thankful Fred remembered his right hand man and best friend this time. It had taken a year, but the boss was finally acknowledging Makwa's innate talents and suitability for the job.

Fred sat down at his desk and pulled out red leather saddlebags from somewhere beneath it. "The crew that logged the area just south last season sent some scouts of their own up into the part of our holdings I'm sending you to survey. There are three locations already pinpointed on the maps. Now, Paul, I need to be clear that you perfectly understand everything I'm saying."

"I, uh, understand everything perfectly, sir."

Fred nodded. "I need you and your crew to set up camps at every location marked on this map."

"What if we arrive and these, uh, are not the best locations for making camp?"

The boss narrowed his eyes, then lifted his hat to run a hand through thin scraggles of gray hair. "Paul. You said you understood."

"Yes... yes. I am sorry, Fred. Camps must be built on the three spots marked."

"There. See? It's easy." He slipped a single map from one of the two identical packs and passed it to Paul. "Look at that."

Paul held the weathered map paper in both hands and studied it. He'd been expecting fresh maps with the newest data from the government. Not something that looked so... old. It looked to be at least ten years old and had to have passed through many, many hands. "I see many marks."

"I've outlined the section of land that I'm instructing you to survey. Unlike some other companies around here, we will not overreach into other land holdings. I need you to stick strictly to the section I've assigned."

Paul nodded firmly. "What are the other X marks?"

"Those south or east of your section are camps from previous seasons. They should be empty now, and they'll be torn down and the materials repurposed in the coming season. Stick to your section, focus on your... building your camps. And I want you to build them in order, starting with the easternmost camp, and then moving west. Are you clear?"

"Yes, sir. I will do exactly as instructed. Have faith, I shall return with the full survey and sections properly marked, ready for cutting come November."

All of Fred's nervous energy dissipated, and he sat perfectly still for a moment, his hands steepled in front of him as he stared back at Paul. Rather, it seemed as if he looked through Paul toward some far-distant point.

"Eh, boss?"

Fred shook as if startled, then put on that typical fake smile of his and tipped his head slightly. "Go and do good work, Paul. The entire company is counting on you. You know that, right?"

Paul returned the smile, but all he could think was, *What an odd thing to say. Success has never really hinged on the preparatory work completed by a land-looker.*

Though it was his first season as land-looker and camp boss, he had plenty of years under his belt in every position in the camps except cook and cookee. From cutting and sawing to bucking and hogging, he'd learned it all and emerged as a leader among men. Even though he couldn't fluently speak any language but his own Canadian version of French, he knew enough of each language common to the diverse jacks to direct them well. Better yet, he knew exactly how to convey what needed to be done, and he could show it better than he could say it. The old bosses called him a natural, born for the ax and for the river, for the snow and the hard edges of the wilderness. Now, it was his turn to be the lumber boss, to manage and supervise, to get things done well, and to give everyone a chance to get paid and make something of their lives.

Most of the party were returning to him from last season, but others he'd been counting on hadn't been seen since the Red Sash Brigade had descended upon the city back in May. It was typical that by September, some men had moved on to other trades, gotten married, taken easier work, or ended up six feet under, if not floating in Saginaw Bay.

On the way to the docks, Paul had picked up Ruby's nephew Thomas—who was practically her son, considering she'd raised him since her sister died in childbirth—from a meeting spot just outside of Hell's Half Mile. He had sent a boy ahead with a message to change the meeting place, and the kid had delivered it just in time. He learned

Ruby had to sneak out quickly and quietly with Thomas, avoiding her boss so he wouldn't protest. The hand off was successful.

Ruby did not cry in front of the boy, but her bloodshot eyes hinted at her pain and worry. To Thomas, she instructed, "Now you be a good young man and listen to everything Mr. Fournier tells you, ya hear?"

"Yes, ma'am," Thomas said solemnly, nodding as he held her gaze. His fists clenched at his sides, and the muscles in his young face were hard. He gave her the lightest hug when she embraced him. Paul pretended not to notice how fiercely the boy blinked back tears.

"I love you, Thomas. You know that, right?"

"Yes, ma'am." He stretched up on his tiptoes, and Ruby met him part way so he could whisper in her ear.

She smiled, then took off his hat to kiss his hair. Thomas's face turned bright red, and he glanced sidelong at Paul.

"Wait over there by that cart." The boy did as Ruby asked, and she turned to Paul. "Promise..." She held one hand against her mouth and tipped her face down, hiding behind the brim of her stylish, lace-trimmed black hat. After sucking in a breath, she lifted her chin again, regaining her proud countenance. "Please, Paul. Please promise me you'll bring him safely back to me."

Paul hesitated. Something in the wind caught his breath. The scent of fresh pine and dug earth struck him suddenly, and it felt like a warning. But it was foolish to feel any such thing. He'd worked this country for five years with few incidents of any note, aside from common lumber camp deaths and accidents, or the river hog drownings in the spring. Sure, he'd seen some strange things; all the jacks had. Nobody talked about them though, and everyone knew that as long as they stuck together, they wouldn't have to worry.

He pushed the feeling aside and forced himself to nod with confidence. "Of course. He'll be safe in the cook shack with Makwa's sisters, and surely he will learn a thing or two to show you when we return."

"Thank you, Paul." Her words came out in a whisper. She sniffled, waved to the boy one last time, then spun on her heel and strode off toward the saloon.

Once her petite form disappeared into the crowd, Paul turned his gaze on the boy. "Come. We cannot be late for the ferry."

Thomas quickly proved to be a quiet boy, but a sharp one too. He studied people with a keen eye, and his head was on a swivel, constantly surveying the world around him. Paul never had to remind him to keep close; the boy stayed right on Paul's heels, just to his left and a step behind. Whatever he'd been through so far in his young life had been cruel enough to make him paranoid.

When they reached the docks, Paul found a group of people waiting on the Third Street Dock exactly where he'd assigned them to meet him. Makwa spotted him first and whispered to the others, causing them to fall silent.

"Is everyone here?" Paul looked over his crew. Ten men, two women, and the boy, Thomas. He already knew most of the men, having been on crews with them over the past three seasons and knew they were ready to work hard. The women would handle the cooking and the laundry, and Thomas would work for them. At least for now, these women would only serve the scouting party, and then maybe smaller camps in the winter. In season, the cooks were mostly men, at least in the big camps Paul had worked in. But these ladies were both women of good repute and, most importantly, the sisters of Makwa, Paul's trail master. His given name was from his Odawa mother, but being raised in Cross Village, his Catholic teachers had assigned Samuel as his Christian name. He and his sisters had been sent out into the world, and together they wandered the north lands in search of honest work as their elders had instructed. The siblings would not—and could not—be separated until the women were suitably married off.

In the past week, Paul had uncovered a niggling pit of worry burrowing in his stomach, the origin of which he could not determine. Was it because he was finally the boss? Or that he'd been selected as the land-looker? After long consideration of the job ahead and studying the maps of the new territory into which they'd be delving for the survey, Paul decided he needed a few more men than the ten he'd originally asked for. Once he'd received approval from Fred, he sent word through the town.

Yet today, only two new faces stared back at him, and there was only an hour left before they were to set off on their journey. Not enough time to round up anyone else.

The first of the newcomers was Eddie, a young man, a teen still, but orphaned and desperately in need of work. Clearly, he'd lied about his age to make a few greenbacks and feed himself.

To Paul's shock, the second face wasn't new at all. The giant of a man hovering a head and a half above all the others and standing before him now was none other than Silver Jack.

"No," Paul said, rubbing his temples with both hands. "*Merde.* Why are you here?"

Jack grinned like a wolf. "Fred asked me to help you."

Cut and Get Out

Silver Jack greeted Paul with a toothy grin and a handshake. "I heard yer needin' more men for timber scoutin'."

"You are up for the work?" Paul didn't know if he trusted the man entirely, and was sure he could go without him if he had to. Whenever they had crossed each other's paths during the weeks that followed the fight, Silver Jack would tip his head, offering a modicum of respect he'd given to no one else. Once, he had even smiled.

Paul's healing knuckles and achy limbs warned him to be careful around the brute.

"I'm here, ain't I? You'll find no better man with an ax."

Makwa, who appeared beside Paul as silently as a ghost, laughed low and hollow and pointed to Paul. "You're talking to the best ax man in the territories. Besides, we don't need ax men. We need survey men, those good with maps and marking trees, and we need men who can build camp."

"I'm all that too," Jack insisted. "I can even make my letters. Can you?"

Makwa snorted. "Of course."

Jack returned his gaze to Paul. "If you'll have me, I'm ready, able, and willing. I'll be no trouble."

Paul nodded, though he didn't really have a say in the matter. "We depart in two hours. Your affairs are in order?" Jack nodded, so he turned to the rest of the group and said, "That question goes for everyone. Stay here, or if you have last-minute business, at least stay out of Hell and her saloons, or you might end up floating face down in the river instead of on the ferry with us."

And, to Jack's credit, he didn't even look back toward town. He remained dockside with the rest of the crew, their breaths puffing in the chill air as they waited.

To Paul's great relief, no one budged. Makwa and his sisters, Awan and Kimi, had brought the wagons he and Paul had packed up yesterday, and everyone seemed ready to get on the ferry. He tried not to stare too often at Awan, but he'd secretly held a flame for her since the first day they'd met. She was beautiful, intelligent, well-spoken, and fluent in three languages. Her graceful movements were ghost-like, and she seemed to float rather than walk, adding to her mystique.

He was glad for her presence, but he couldn't deny that she also distracted him.

The sooner they set off, the better. Unlike winter lumberin', the survey expedition paid the same no matter how long it took. Well, unless there were extenuating circumstances, like mineral discoveries.

Paul shook his head. "Makwa, Jack. As soon as the ferry master lets us on, lead the crew in loading up the wagons and the horses."

After ensuring everyone knew their job—and with young Thomas still by his side—Paul prepared the blank contracts he'd brought along for whomever might answer his late-hour call for survey men. Then he had Eddie and Jack sign their names after reading.

They loaded their supplies onto the steamer along with two wagons, four horses needed to draw them, and two more workhorses as a backup in case any fell sick or injured. Of the two additional horses, one was Makwa's gray morgan, Kitchi, and the other was Bébé, Paul's blue roan percheron and morgan cross mare. The wagons held tools, canvas tents, a cook stove, cookware, and all the materials they couldn't get out in the wild forests of Saginaw Country.

Makwa's sisters were the first to be settled, taking a spot near the front of the steamer and watching the water while whispering almost inaudibly to one another. They kept their distance, and Paul respected that. The men worked together to finish loading up the wagons and horses, then took turns caring for them during the trip.

By water, they would travel to Oscoda, and from there, overland past last season's clear-cut forests. The journey was simple, but Paul still kept a careful eye on his crew. He had a history with steamers and fights, though that usually only happened when he was off the job. Still, the ships made him uneasy, and it never hurt to keep himself awake and alert. Some men dozed, others leaned on the railing and stared out over the waves. Thomas wandered between the horses and the railing of the steamer, never saying a single word until Paul offered him bread and an apple. The boy thanked Paul, then found a place away from others to sit alone and savor the simple meal.

Makwa spent most of his time near the prow, speaking with his sisters in their native tongue. Paul wasn't sure why, but he was glad the mission school hadn't beaten their language out of them. Some schools in the mission towns scattered around what should have been New France were home to dark and brutal reputations.

He supposed that the appreciation of holding onto one's native language had something to do with his love of his own mother tongue: *français*. Whether or not it was true to the Old World, it was the tongue of his family, of his people, going back to when his great-grandfather had come as a fur trader, a *coureur des bois*. The man had decided he liked the New World so much that he took a native wife who'd been among his guides and settled down.

Paul was a child of the woods, like that old man he'd never met, and like his great-grandmother and her people. The forests ran deep in his veins, and he often wondered if that was to blame for his rough edges and wild ways. He stared out over the white-capped waves of Lake Huron as he thought of the job ahead, recalling the marks on the map and the strange conversation with Fred Langley.

The late September sun had burned away all the mist and fog by the time they reached the docks at Oscoda. In an efficiency that spoke to the group's collective experience, they disembarked with the horses and the wagons, then double-checked all of their supplies and ensured everything was tightly secured and ready for hard trails. Paul seated Thomas in the back of a wagon, then inhaled deeply as he took in the new but bustling coastal town. As the smell of wood smoke overwhelmed the clean, cool breeze off Lake Huron, Paul swallowed hard against the thirst for a hard, stomach-burning drink. Even in a town established only fourteen years earlier, there was drinkable whiskey and cards to be played. He took a final headcount before ordering his party down a street leading west out of town.

From well-worn dirt roads to overgrown trails, Makwa scouted ahead as they ventured deeper into the desolate wilderness. As trail master, he ensured the paths ahead could handle their wagons, found shallow crossings, and avoided the swampiest areas where they could easily get stuck. Watching the man disappear into the distance always made Paul a little nervous, and that nervousness wouldn't be relieved until Makwa reappeared later.

The only sounds accompanying them along the trail today were the squeaks and groans of the wagons, the thump of the horses' hooves against the rock and dirt of the trail, and the occasional snort or whinny. A spoken word was rare and came only from Makwa when he returned to share his discoveries or when Paul barked orders to the crew. All the others kept their thoughts to themselves as they trudged along down the trail or rode in the wagons.

Paul didn't want to snap at the crew, but the farther west they rode, the more frayed his nerves became, and every word came out harsher than he intended. No one else seemed to notice the indiscernible creatures moving in the distance ahead. Shadows darting between stumps and behind hills. Mere coyotes, he was sure, but the idea didn't ease his mind.

Miles and miles of scarred stumps greeted them, interspersed by the occasional copse of recent growth, mostly bramble berry bushes, along with oak and poplar saplings. The logging companies had snapped up the vast majority of the land in the north country in vast tracts. Nearly everything they could see to the horizon and the gently rounded tops of far-away hills was owned by the lumber companies, whose unofficial motto was "cut and get out." They took all they could, stripping the land of its finest resources then absconded from the state with the green-gold wealth its trees had generated.

To gain that enormous wealth and leave with it, the lumber companies willingly risked and sacrificed many of the lives of immigrants and outsiders, men and boys who had no families, or whose families hadn't the power to command justice for the dead.

Still, logging offered wages that were a far sight better than any of these men (and a few women) could make in most other trades, or back home in the distant reaches whence they'd come. So, every season, they said their prayers, swung their axes, and rode the logs down the rivers and Great Lakes back to Bay City and Saginaw. What the company hadn't taken from their season's wages through company store purchases, the jacks would inevitably spend in two weeks of drinking, gambling, and attention from saloon girls.

If Paul could stay out of Hell's Half Mile, he might save enough money to apprentice in a safer trade and start a family someday. But the lure of that section of Bay City was too tempting, too distracting, and he couldn't quit the cards, the whiskey, and the company of ladies that frequented those places.

Yet he couldn't forget Langley's warning. Maybe restrictions came with promotions, and this was part of the territory for a land-looker. He aimed to be lumber boss come November, and if that meant giving up his favorite pastimes, he'd do it.

Just before it had become too dark, he finally started to see full forests again. After a quick consultation of his maps by lantern light, Paul figured they still had another half-day of travel ahead of them before they could make the first base camp.

It was too far still to push on into the darkness, risking injury to his people, horses, or wagons. It might have been his first season as lumber boss, but it was his fifth season scoutin' and fellin'. There was always the risk inherent in the work: every season in timber country could be one's last, whether from accidents, malice, or the wild things of the woodlands.

Paul mentally chewed over the detriment of his vices as the sun dipped into the west ahead of them, hovering closer and closer to that distant, fuzzy green horizon. He called for his crew to make camp near a deep-running, ice-cold creek. It would make for an excellent source of water they could drink from.

Steeling his resolve, he watched over his crew—his men, women, and young Thomas—as they set up a quick camp. First season as boss or not, he wouldn't lose any souls, not during this expedition, nor in felling season either.

Sometimes They Look Like Wolves

Makwa returned from gathering a second load of wood just as the crew had finished raising three tents: a small one for Makwa and his sisters, and two larger tents to split between the rest of the men. Awan and Kimi had a fire roaring and water boiling by the time the men finished setting up the rest of camp and then began the work of plucking and preparing to cook the two turkeys Makwa had hunted earlier in the day while scouting.

When there was nothing left to be done but wait for dinner and watch the fire, Paul pulled out a chunk of oak from his satchel along with his carving knife and got to work at it, slicing away as he watched his men go about their assigned duties. He'd assigned the two youngest men to care for the horses. Another pair of youngins he expected might be proved flunkies come November, so he set them and Thomas to assisting the women, hopeful they might learn a thing or two about the women's efficient way of cleaning and their secrets to making a flavorful meal from so little. The rest of the men, seasoned or not, brought back armfuls of wood for the fire and chopped it or worked in the tent, laying out pallet beds of evergreen boughs and each man's many layers of bedroll blankets.

It wasn't long before everyone had finished their assigned tasks and gathered around the fire, loosening up after drinking their fill from the creek and resting their tired bodies near the warmth. Conversation started slowly, but once it got going, it couldn't be stopped. Paul encouraged the crew to talk, hoping it would build the bonds that would get them through the survey quickly. He tempered their volume and any arguments with his steely gaze and simple, hard words.

He needed to ensure the women always felt safe and welcome. Not only was it proper, but he'd rather not have any of his small crew set to cooking if they chased away Makwa's sisters with bad manners. The thought of merely disappointing Awan needled at Paul's pride. Sure, these were rough men, but there was a code to maintain, like that of the knights from the Old World. To Paul, those stories were his guiding thread through the dark maze of life: be kind to women and children, defend the defenseless, give with a generous heart, walk the world as an honest man, and fight for what he believed in.

Mostly, he fought over whiskey and cards, but he hadn't backed down from a fight yet. Surely, that was something knightly.

"Have any of you not been to these woods yet?" Makwa's voice cut through the low murmur of conversation and through Paul's rambling thoughts.

A few hands rose, all from the youngest men. Paul noticed Thomas kept his hands neatly in his lap, but there was no reason to call him out for not welcoming attention to himself. The boy glanced at Paul, then quickly returned his attention to Makwa.

The last man to slowly raise his hand was Silver Jack.

Paul stared at the man, blinking. "You've never been to Saginaw Country?"

"Hell, I—"

Paul shot him a glare that cut him off and nodded toward the women.

"I mean, I just got to the city in May. I was coming out of Jackson, not outta these woods."

Makwa nodded. "Is it alright to tell them?" he asked Paul.

Paul nodded, finishing the water in his cup and getting up to scoop more from the barrel they'd filled during camp setup.

So Makwa began. "A little over two hundred years ago, the Sauk people who lived in and claimed these lands made a great sin against the Chippewa people of what we now call the Grand Traverse Bay."

"That's where I was born," one of the seasoned men, Jon, interjected. "I know this tale well."

Ignoring the interruption, Makwa continued. "Their sin was capturing a brave and his woman, and taking them as slaves. Many great tribes joined together to destroy the Sauk. Only a few women were spared, exiled to distant tribes."

The seasoned Saginaw men nodded along as Makwa spoke, as if they knew every word of this tale by heart and exactly what the native man would say next.

"But there have remained legends of Sauks who survived. If not Sauk warriors and hunters themselves, then it is their ghosts that have roamed the land for hundreds of years. To this day, they stalk all those who would dare lay claim to this place."

"Ghost stories!" Silver Jack laughed, grinning widely. "I have a couple good ones to share—"

"Not a story," Paul said abruptly. "A warning."

"It is indeed a warning," Makwa confirmed. "No one travels alone in these woods. If you gotta go somewhere, you go in pairs. And if you see something you can't explain, you must return to camp and tell me immediately. We have greater safety in numbers, and we have to stick together when the woods begin to feel strange."

"Yer tellin' me that we have to watch out for ghosts?"

"Dey don't look like ghosts," Paul said, unable to tame his French accent as well as he usually did. "Sometimes, um, they look like wolves or deer. Other times, like people, like any of us here," he gestured around the group, "but... they are never quite right."

He glanced at Thomas and found the boy's eyes so wide they looked as if they'd fall out of his head any second now. Although it pinched at his heart to know the boy was afraid, it was better all around if he kept that fear well-stoked while they were out here. He'd rather have the boy clinging to his leg than out wandering the forest alone for the sake of boredom or curiosity.

"They may even call out to you." Makwa dropped another log onto the fire. "It may sound like someone you know. Or it could sound like your own voice calling back to you."

"Isn't that called an echo?" Lars asked. He was a Swedish youth, hardly old enough to even be called a man. "My English is not so good."

Awan snorted and rolled her eyes.

"Your English is very good, Lars," Makwa reassured the boy. "Yes, when you call out and your own voice comes back to you, that is an echo in places like canyons or caves. We have caves here, small ones, but we don't have canyons. The trees don't normally echo back to us with our own voices, though the waterways can often carry voices fairly far."

Lars nodded as if understanding, yet the look in his eyes told Paul that the boy was still confused. He was simply too proud to say so.

Another young man, Joseph, a French Canadian like Paul himself with a thick accent, asked the question Lars wouldn't. "How do we tell the difference?"

Makwa glanced between the boys, then pointedly around the whole group. "If you call out into the wild, the wild shouldn't call back."

The rest of the night was spent largely in quiet reflection, the mood dampened by Makwa's tale and warning, but Paul wasn't worried. Theirs was serious, deadly work, and there was no room for complacency or gentleness—except for the women, of course.

He ordered them all to bed shortly after Makwa finished his warning tale. Tomorrow would be a long day as well, and they all needed the rest.

Paul was the last one up, ensuring everyone—especially Thomas—followed his instructions. He lay back on the ground and watched the stars as he chewed over Makwa's warning. Remembering the first time he'd heard the tale and how quickly he'd dismissed it. He had come from Hull, a riverside town where eerie lakes, dark forests, and creatures of legend abounded. They were just as ominous, just as threatening, and he'd heard plenty of tales of curses and hauntings passed down through his family from his Algonquin great-grandmother. So he hadn't any reason to believe there could be anything in the Michigan Territory—and Saginaw Country's vast swampland especially—that could shake him.

But he learned that first season, the winter of '65, just how wrong he had been to ignore the warnings. There were things here that no amount of storytelling could prepare you for. Things that haunted a man, slithering through his dreams long after the season. And worse, things that hunted men, and even more so those who came to claim the green gold so abundant: the country's white pine trees that would be hacked apart into planks and shipped out all over the world.

Paul had almost lost his life that first winter, and he would have if not for the watchful eye of a more seasoned man who knew the safer ways through these haunted lands. He'd kept a tight grip on Paul's collar when he'd dared to wander too far afield. Paul could almost see it now, in his memory. The glowing red eyes, the mangy black fur...

A cool breeze washed over Paul, and a shiver crawled down his spine. He instinctively grasped the big hunting knife on his belt as he slowly sat upright and rose to his feet. The fire crackled, and he kept his gaze beyond it, studying the darkness and pockets of shadows at the edges of camp. It was too early along their journey to be this jumpy already, but Makwa's brief story always lit his memory of that first season and the dark creature that had stalked him. The tale brought the things he'd seen back to life in his mind.

Something moved in the darkness to his right, and he spun toward it, knife ready to bite into flesh and bone. He thought of his ax, attached to the side of the main wagon a dozen feet from where he now stood.

A twig snapped behind him, and he whirled, raising his knife.

Only Awan stood before him, frowning as she glanced between the knife and his face. Her deep, dark eyes, wide with more concern than fear, reflected the dancing firelight and the glint of his blade.

"Awan!" He resisted the adrenaline that threatened the steadiness of his hands as he pushed his knife back into its sheath on his belt. "*Je suis désolé!*"

"Hearing things, Mister Fournier?"

He shook his head. "No." He lied, not wanting to frighten her.

"I heard them," she said calmly, taking a few steps forward to stand closer to him. Her voice was so soft it was nearly a whisper as she looked beyond him into the darkness. The sound of her voice felt like a warm spring day to him. He turned to stare at the shadows with her. "They're watching us already. It feels like something more than simple curiosity this time. It feels like..." She paused, as if struggling to find the right words. "Hunger."

The Warning of the Forest

PAUL WOKE ON HABIT early in the morning. Even in season, he was always the first one to rise, and he maintained that standard on every scouting trip. He rose silently, tugged on his boots, struck a match, and slipped out of his tent into the chill, pre-dawn air to light his oil lantern. As he held it aloft, coyotes scampered almost silently out of camp. He surveyed the camp goods, the wagons, and the sleeping horses to find all was well. The small canines likely hadn't ventured close enough to alert the horses, and they hadn't been able to break into anything.

The fire was nearly dead, so Paul tended to it quickly, stoking the glowing embers back to life before adding more kindling and logs. Just enough, he figured, to get them through morning tea and breakfast. Once the fire was roaring and a large pot of water set to boil, he held the lantern high and carefully made his way to the water's edge to perform his morning ablutions.

All the unease he had felt the night before was gone, replaced by the calm and tranquility of dawn in the wild lands. Naught but the burbling of the creek and the chirping of crickets greeted him. Soon, the warblers and chickadees would sing their morning greeting and let him know the sun was coming.

Paul finished his morning routine with quiet prayers, then headed back into the heart of camp to wake his crew. By the time he finished, Makwa and his sisters had already completed their morning ablutions and were sitting by the fire, sipping the tea Paul had prepared. Thomas sat between Awan and Kimi, and Paul felt a little tension lift from his shoulders.

"Morning," Silver Jack greeted the camp as he walked back from the creek.

Everyone around the fire returned the greeting in some form or another, from nods and grunts to verbal responses, each crew member in various states of alertness.

Breakfast was a simple meal: biscuits and bacon, which had been bought in Bay City the day before. Some ate quickly, and others, like Makwa and his sisters, savored their breakfast. Paul fell somewhere in between, eating while checking supplies and directing his men to pack up. A bite of bacon here, an order to his men there, and soon enough, they were mounting up on horses and in wagons, and hitting the trail.

As soon as his sisters were settled, Makwa lit out on his horse, Kitchi, to scout ahead. His tasks were crucial: marking the trail ahead for the wagons and finding the best potential campsites of those marked at the end of the previous season.

The rest of the day passed uneventfully, and the farther they traveled, the denser the forests became to the north side of their westerly trail until they reached their assigned sections of Langley Lumber Company's untouched virgin forests of Saginaw Country. Those mighty trees stood tall and thick with sparse undergrowth, swaying heavily in the breeze and casting dancing sunlight and shadow on the forest floor.

He headed them toward the farthest point marked on the map, despite his instructions from Langley. That man had never laid a hand on an ax or stayed longer than a few hours in a lumber camp. Langley couldn't understand the process and pressures of the land-looker. He knew how to hire the people to do the work; he didn't know how to do the work. Paul preferred to take the approach he'd been taught supporting previous surveys: work west to east, so at the end of building the camps, they'd be closer to Lake Huron and the ferry that would bring them home. It was more efficient than the way Langley wanted it done, and the older man would be none the wiser.

The way Paul figured it, as long as he got the job done, the *how* didn't matter.

"We're nearly there," Paul reassured his team. He'd let Thomas ride at the front of the saddle with him for a couple of miles, but now he lifted the boy to the back of the wagon again so he could look at his map. The document was clearly marked and matched the terrain. Even if it hadn't been, Paul was familiar enough with the area from the previous season.

Makwa rode up as they stopped the wagons at the end of the trail worn into the earth from last season. "Two river branches flow to the Au Sable, so we have options."

"And the terrain?"

"Rough. There's a lot of swampland and plenty of deadfalls."

"Did you spot any good areas for rollways?"

"Yes," Makwa responded without hesitation. "The creeks and river cut deep into the land. Wherever it's not flat marsh, there are large bluffs to be found."

"To start, we need a base camp, a place we can reach with the wagons."

"I've found a place to start. Looks like it was used as a camp before. Flat ground, right next to a deep creek. And it's only about four miles west of here."

Paul considered as he returned his gaze to his map. "We need to set up several camps this year. Let us make our trail to the first location."

Makwa turned his horse west again and headed down the stark tree line, the wagons following behind him. The ground was already well trodden, and it was easy to see where last year's work had been cut off. Though their path was soft and overgrown, it was already set—at least for this part of their journey. Paul knew it wouldn't be that way for long. As soon as they entered the great woods, there wouldn't be a simple path through the trees, especially for the wagons. Though Michigan wasn't a mountainous state, the wilderness hid gullies and gorges, ridges and great pits, and ancient mountains that had long ago been worn down by wind, water, time, and glaciers.

After traveling nearly three miles along the tree line, their path diminished to little more than a wide game trail. Paul motioned for the wagons to stop, then dismounted from Bébé to stretch his legs and consider the route Makwa wanted them to take. The trees were tight, but it was as if a little tunnel had been crafted especially for them, with just enough room for the wagons to get through beneath the curving limbs of branches thick with leaves. Birds chirped, chipmunks and squirrels chittered, and throughout the undergrowth, movement stirred, life carried on.

The trail extended as far as Paul could see, only slightly curving here or there, but before long becoming indistinguishable from the rest of the forest. "How far does it go?"

Makwa shrugged. "Won't know until we follow it. We can hope it goes all the way to the south branch of the Au Sable."

Paul mounted his horse again, tapped his heels against the mare's sides, then motioned for the wagons to follow.

Silver Jack, who had been unusually quiet on the trail, was the driver of the lead wagon. He let Thomas settle between himself and the shotgun rider before picking up the harness reins and rapping them gently against the horses' backs. They started forward, the wagon jerking into motion, and he turned them onto the trail as Makwa cantered around and took the lead once more.

But as Paul followed and rode beneath the elaborate threshold of the as-yet uncut forest, a sharp, frigid wind blew past, taking his cap off his head. Shocked cries rang out as the sudden gust struck each wagon full of people. Even the horses gave nervous whinnies, and Makwa's horse, Kitchi, reared, her eyes rolling as she fought with him to get back to the rest of the group. Finally, he gave the mare her head and let her race back to the wagons, where she danced and blew harshly through flared nostrils.

Paul held the reins tight as Bébé danced beneath him, trotting nervously and side-stepping away as Kitchi came thundering back.

Aside from the pounding of the spooked horses' hooves, Paul detected an oddness around them. At first, he couldn't pinpoint the source, but when he did, his pulse began thundering in his ears. All the sounds of the forest creatures had stopped when they crossed under the natural archway. The birds no longer sang, and squirrels and chipmunks no longer chittered. All movement in the underbrush ceased. A chill crawled down Paul's spine as he listened to the warning of the forest, carried by the undercurrent of the creaking trunks of the trees and the shuffling moan of the wind through their branches.

"Back up!" he shouted, but the rising wind stole his words. Paul gestured firmly for the drivers to back up, and they calmly complied, retreating out of the forest and returning onto the path at its perimeter. The horses tossed their heads, nervous, snorting, and unsteady, as they finally obeyed the reins. The second wagon backed out first, then turned and pulled forward beyond the path and the more southerly side of the trail. Paul helped guide the lead wagon, resisting the urge to rush them. If they hurried, they might scare the horses even more, and he didn't want them bolting or getting injured in their harnesses.

Paul gritted his teeth against the strange feeling tickling his senses and spoke soothingly to the horses as he backed them out of the forest and onto the main trail. "Shhhh. Ooolllaaa. *Calme*."

As soon as the lead wagon was out, Paul and Makwa following close behind, Paul felt like he could take a full breath again. The wind faded to a calming breeze, and the songs of the birds and the intermittent chatter of the wildlife returned. Somehow, the sky seemed dimmer than when they'd entered only a few minutes before, and the sun now hung lower in the sky.

Paul flexed his fingers against the reins, his knuckles sore from holding them so tightly and fighting to keep Bébé under control. It couldn't be right. He covered his eyes and studied the position of the sun in the sky.

"Paul," Makwa said as he rubbed Kitchi's trembling neck. "Something is wrong."

"*Oui*. That is clear, *mon ami*."

The rest of the crew muttered in low tones to one another, all the while staring at Paul, awaiting his instructions and reassurance.

"The trail is too narrow," he lied, then more softly asked Makwa, "Is there a place outside the forest where we can camp? A place near water?"

"Yes. We passed a spot a half mile back where the south branch dips out of the forest."

"We will go east and make camp near the river," Paul shouted, gesturing back the way they'd come.

"Much farther east, and we'll be back in Oscoda," Makwa muttered as he drew up close to Paul.

"Should we risk the forest again? No. We will set up camp. You and I will scout ahead for the next camp."

Makwa clenched his jaw and nodded, then put his heels to Kitchi's sides and rode ahead to lead the crew to the spot he'd picked along the river.

Paul's tension eased a little as they rode east again, though the feeling of being watched remained. The squeaking of the wheels and bumpy ride soothed the questions, pounding out a beat in his head. The sounds and his thoughts melded together like a discordant lullaby, rhythmic and set to the beat of the horses' hooves. Soon he dozed, reins in one hand and the other resting on the pommel of his saddle.

Visions flashed through his mind, reminders of the things he had seen in his first season all those long winters ago. Teeth, fur, glowing red eyes peering at him from the deepest shadows. Growling that shook one's spine, wisps of darkness that appeared to move faster than possible. The feeling of being watched, the sensation he felt even now crawling up his spine as he wavered between the conscious and unconscious worlds.

It's Right There

"Woah!" Makwa shouted, his voice sounding far away.

Paul's eyes flew open, and he shook himself awake. He shivered as he sat up straighter, that feeling of being watched clinging to his skin like wet clothes. It wasn't like him to doze off during the day, especially not while leading his crew. Maybe he'd gotten too lax between seasons. Though he'd still worked as a carpenter, life was considerably more relaxed when one basked in civilization.

The wagons had stopped, and his horse and the pack horses had pulled up behind them. They knew their job and were used to traveling in single file, always remaining with the herd.

Paul skirted the second wagon—formerly the lead wagon when they were headed west—and halted at the front. Silver Jack sat in the driver's seat, his hands gripping reins that now rested on his knees. His eyes were closed, and his chest rose and fell slowly with gentle breaths.

Fast asleep, as was the man riding shotgun, and Thomas between them.

"*Sapristi!* Did no one sleep last night?"

Silver Jack jolted awake, did a double take when he spotted the crew boss, then poked his shotgun rider with a thick index finger. "I was just restin' my eyes, Paul. I swear it!"

"I can see that, Jack." Paul held eye contact through a few tense moments and watched Jack's face redden. Then he clicked his tongue and rode to the front of the next wagon. Glancing back over his shoulder, he said to Jack, "Hold here 'til I say."

Jack fumed silently, anger flashing in his eyes but embarrassment apparent in his cheeks. He picked up the reins and deferred to Paul with a brief nod. At least he hadn't tried to insist that he'd been awake the entire time. Under normal circumstances, Paul might have torn into the man, but he had a feeling today's events were anything but normal.

Paul found the driver and shotgun rider of the first wagon just as drowsy as those in the previous one. All the passengers in the back slept deeply, unaware that they had stopped at all.

He even found Makwa slumped in his saddle.

Beyond, a small, gurgling branch of the Au Sable River arched southward out of the uncut forest, cutting sharply around a bend before winding north and then easterly again.

"We make camp here," Paul barked the command, then dismounted his horse. He made for the creek and knelt down at the edge before splashing his face with the icy water. The fog of sleep still clouded his mind and sat like lead in his muscles.

The rest of the crew followed his lead, trudging in a slow procession toward the water to wake themselves. As they became more alert, Paul directed them to set up camp, ensuring everything was positioned the way he liked it. The temporary camp would be close to the river while still leaving a wide swath of access to it for the sturdier camp they would build over the coming week. Once everyone got to work, the tents went up within the hour, and the women had a fire roaring with tea ready and a stew started over the flames.

It should have only been late afternoon, but the sun already threatened to dip below the tree line to their west.

"Where has the time gone?" Paul accepted a cup of tea from Kimi and stood beside the fire. He watched the salted pork and beans cook in the pot and enjoyed the fragrance of the herbs as Awan added them. She directed Thomas to stir, gently, and the boy did as instructed. With only a little seasoning and sparse rations, the women had already started off the expedition with a town-worthy meal.

"When will we scout the trail?" Makwa sidled up beside him, also accepting a tin cup filled to the brim and steaming.

"*Demain.* It will be dark soon. You and I will leave at dawn."

"Good. I—"

"Mr. Fournier?" Thomas asked, still stirring the stew.

"*Oui?*"

"Will I be going with you tomorrow?"

Paul shook his head. "You will stay here to help Awan and Kimi."

The boy turned his gaze on the stew, but his spoon stopped stirring. "Aunt Ruby said... well, sir, she said I'd stay right with you. Instructed me to do so."

Something pinched in Paul's chest. "You will be where I think you are safest, Thomas. I made a promise to Ruby, yes? I promised to keep you safe. Tomorrow, you will be safest here in camp."

"Is there something dangerous in the forest?"

"Yes," Makwa jumped in. "Wolves, big cats, bears, wolverines. There are many dangerous creatures in the old forest. You're safest here at camp."

The boy's eyes darted to the darkness pooling between the trees on the north side of the creek as the last light of day was swallowed by the glittering evening sky. "Are... Are you sure?"

Makwa said nothing, but a tingle crawled across Paul's scalp, raising the hairs on the back of his neck.

He fought the unusual anxiety pulling at his mind, like a dog chewing at the frayed edges of a worn rug. Of course it would be fine. Better than fine. Thomas needed to stay here. There was safety in numbers, and the greater number of the crew would stay in camp. "*Oui,* Thomas. I am sure."

"Well," Makwa added quickly, rubbing the back of his neck with one hand. "As soon as I finish dinner, I'll be ready to sleep. I feel like we traveled ten times the distance we actually covered today."

Paul nodded in agreement but kept his gaze on Thomas, watching as the boy filled bowls of stew and passed them out. The bowls were accepted without enthusiasm.

Everyone felt that same strange exhaustion, but no one gave voice or credence to their mutual understanding. It was something a person pushed to the back of their mind, not ignoring it entirely, but enough to continue on in life without daring to uncover some disturbing inconsistency about the world surrounding them.

Dinner was quiet, and even the usual fast eaters took more time with their bowls of salted pork and beans than they usually would have. Paul sat with them, perched on an overturned barrel, chewing slowly and quietly. Without fail, he always chewed with his mouth closed, conscious of the most noticeable of his unusual traits: a double row of teeth, both upper and lower. When spotted, people stared in awe, disgust, or fright, and it always sparked a red-hot anger in him. Better to keep his mouth closed and speak as few words as possible.

When he'd shooed everyone off to bed, Paul threw a few extra logs on the fire and cleaned up the edges, ensuring anything flammable was well away in case any embers fell out.

He took one last look around the camp, ready to fall into bed inside his tent, when he spotted Awan sitting on a thick log with her back to the fire and staring northward.

He walked up beside her. "Something wrong?"

She turned to him, staring up with her pretty dark eyes, then returned her gaze to the darkness. "We all feel it. This season is different."

He nodded, even though she wasn't looking at him. "We will be fine. Stick together, go nowhere alone."

Awan said nothing as she watched the inky black shadows stretching beyond the reach of the fire's light.

"Not going to bed yet?"

"I am not."

"*Bonne nuit*, then."

Paul dreamed of darkness, of trees bending their boughs and lashing wildly at him. The skies were open and rain drenched the world, sweeping him out in a great flood. Something wrapped around his ankles and yanked him downward. He fought for the surface, straining with his arms and kicking with his legs against whatever held him.

He freed himself and broke the surface, only to be struck by wave after wave.

They tossed him, rolled him under the crests, and the current pulled him farther from shore. He strained, his muscles tired, and righted himself, ducking under the waves and bobbing along the surface where he could. Looking around, he saw nothing but water. There were no trees, no far-off hills, no sandy bluffs... no shoreline.

Lightning split the sky above him, and soul-shaking thunder clapped and rolled. He tried to stay calm, but he didn't know which way to swim. A slithering tendril wound its way around one ankle, and this time Paul couldn't shake it. He fought again, but his muscles were tired, his limbs so heavy. The thing yanked him again, and he no longer fought as it pulled him down into the watery depths of Lake Huron.

"Mr. Fournier!" A hissing whisper jolted Paul from the nightmare.

He sprang upright and sat there heaving in ragged breaths, drenched in sweat and trembling. The dream had felt so real, and it was the first time he remembered giving up the fight.

Paul ran an unsteady hand through his short-cut hair and focused on slowing his breaths. Five counts in, five counts out.

"Mr. Paul?"

Despite the darkness, there was enough ambient light for Paul to see Thomas crouched beside the pallet. His young eyes were wide with fear and filled with worry, and his arms were wrapped around himself.

"What is it?"

"I'm sorry to wake you," Thomas said, his whisper barely audible. "But I have to... go."

"Go? Go where?"

"Outside."

"Why on earth would you need to go outside?"

"To... um... Well, Silver Jack called it 'watering the bushes'."

"*Maudit!* I am sorry, Thomas. *Allons-y.*" Paul got up, but the boy simply stared up at him in confusion.

"Allan zee?"

"*Allons-y.* It is French, and it is how we say 'let's go'."

The boy rose and followed Paul silently out of the tent. A chorus of crickets met their ears outside the tent. Their chirping was both loud and gently soothing. It was one of Paul's favorite sounds, a swan song lullaby for the end of summer.

Paul lit one lantern and gestured toward the far edge of camp, away from the tents and the water.

Thomas stared up at him, as if waiting for something.

"Come, boy," Paul urged, but the child didn't budge. "Come, come."

Thomas swallowed hard, and only moved from the spot he'd been glued to when Paul raised his lantern high enough to better light the area. He trotted after Paul toward the very edge of the circle of light in the camp, then hurried to do his business.

Without saying a word, he turned and trotted back toward the fire.

"Slow," Paul urged in a low voice. "I do not want you to trip and fall face-first into the fire!"

Thomas stopped in front of the entrance to their tent and turned back toward Paul. His face was half in shadow and half-lit from the low-burning campfire. His eyes bulged, and he raised one hand, pointing a finger toward Paul.

Swift chills swept through Paul, and the hairs on the back of his neck stood on end, but he controlled himself.

It was nothing. Just a boy's overactive imagination combined with his fear of the wilderness.

A branch cracked in the darkness behind Paul, and he whirled, holding the lantern high in his left hand. The fingers of his right hand curled into a fist, ready to land hell's blows onto anything that dared meet him.

But nothing came at him. No wolf lunging for his throat or a bear rushing to maul him. The prickling sensation of being watched washed over him, raising goosebumps on his skin. He moved the lantern in an arc, searching for whatever might have made the noise, but the shadows were thick on this moonless night and seemed to repel his light.

Paul stepped slowly backward, breathing shallow and staying ready in case something leaped from the shadows.

He kept going like that, step by agonizing step, until he stood between the darkness and Thomas.

"I don't see anything," Paul said. "Go inside the tent and go back to sleep."

"You don't see it?"

He broke his gaze from the shadows beyond the ring of campfire light and peered down at the boy. "See what? No. I see only shadows."

"There…" Thomas pointed again, his eyes brimming with tears and arm trembling.

Paul turned and squinted at the darkness, holding the lantern high again.

Amongst the shadows, he could only make out the sharp ends of broken branches, prickly bunches of pine needles, and thick tree trunks.

"It's right there!" Thomas insisted, his voice low but strangled, choking on the simple words.

After dimming the lantern and blinking his eyes several times to clear them, Paul looked again. Two thin skeletal antlers topped the mangy head of a creature Paul had tried so hard to forget. He couldn't make out all the details, but he knew what it was. He could sense its malice.

His blood ran cold and his breath caught in his chest when he made out the faintly glowing red eyes staring straight into his own. He could see the intelligence in those eyes, the knowing, the understanding of all that was, all that is, and all that would come.

Paul wanted to reach for his ax. It was only a few strides closer to the fire, leaning against the overturned barrel he'd sat on for dinner. But Thomas…

Every instinct in Paul's being told him to fight, to charge into bloody battle with the creature. But before he could decide on how to protect Thomas *and* retrieve his ax, the creature sank back into the shadows and vanished. A twig snapped, and after another second, a tree groaned and fell, crashing away from them somewhere in the forest.

The creature was gone now, and Paul could feel it in his bones as the enchantment broke, but he hoped the damn thing hadn't woken everyone else in the camp with its exit.

Thorns, Thistles, and Crawling Spiders

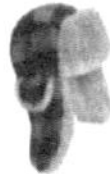

To his surprise, no one had woken the night before when the tree had fallen in the forest. After calming Thomas, Paul got them both to bed. Paul had lain mostly still, rarely sleeping as he stared up into the darkness through the rest of the early morning hours. When he could no longer lie there sleepless, Paul dressed, grabbed his lantern, and struck his match outside the tent to light it. He looked around, suspicious, careful. When nothing moved and the shadows yielded only the empty quiet of pre-dawn, Paul moved through camp and went about his morning tasks.

The campfire still burned, albeit low and quiet, and proved easy to stoke. He headed to the creek for his ablutions and returned to put the kettle on. Afterward, he roused the camp, calling the men to start the day and prepare his scouting kit. Joseph and Lars completed their morning rituals quickly and tended to the horses, taking each to the river to drink and then feeding them. On Paul's orders, they fed, watered, and saddled Kitchi and Bébé. All the while, Paul studied his maps and marked the day's points of interest.

Foremost in his thoughts was the game trail they'd been spooked off the day before. He gently folded his maps, returned them to his satchel, and prepared the red leather saddlebags Fred Langley had given him. Once that was done, he sat by the fire, gladly accepting a bowl of the bacon and oatmeal that Awan and Kimi had prepared with the help of the future flunkies.

Makwa and Paul were the first to finish eating breakfast, and as they set off toward their horses, Silver Jack jumped up from his seat and almost dropped his tin bowl into the fire.

"You're headin' out then?" he asked before gobbling a giant spoonful of his oatmeal. "Bring me wit' ya."

Paul and Makwa glanced at each other. Jack shoved the rest of his bacon into his mouth as he watched them.

"I would like for you to stay here and help build the first base camp." Paul put his cap on his head, tossed his saddlebags over his left shoulder, and leaned his double-bit ax over his right shoulder.

Makwa moved closer and whispered in Paul's ear. "This time, it might not be a bad idea to have another man with us."

Paul mulled it over. He hated changing his mind, especially after he'd already spoken his intentions in front of the crew. "Fine. Saddle up fast. We are leaving now."

Jack slurped the last of his oatmeal from the bowl before Kimi took it from him. He thanked her around a full mouth, then darted into a tent to grab his things.

"Lars, saddle a horse for him, *s'il vous plaît*." Paul then waved to the rest of the camp. "Keep safe, watch for wolves, and get to work clearing the area and cutting lumber for our cook shack. *Compris?*"

"Yes, boss," they answered collectively in a mishmash of accents, but all with eagerness to get started. The sooner the cook shack was up and running, the better their meals would be, and that would motivate any man despite the strangeness of the previous day.

Paul and Makwa started off down the trail, and only five minutes had passed when Jack finally caught up to them, galloping up on a chestnut Belgian.

"Woah!" He kept his voice low and calming as he brought the Belgian from an urgent canter down to a jolting trot, then a walk, when he slowed on Paul's left. "Thanks for letting me come along, boss."

"Why?" Paul kept his eyes mostly forward, though he peered into the wood line from time to time.

"Well, bein' honest, I just want ta know what happened yesterday. Were there snakes on the trail? A panther, or maybe a bear?"

"I suppose we shall find out."

Makwa walked his horse to Paul's right, closest to the wood line bordering the north side of the trail. His gaze remained on that forest they'd soon enter. "I haven't seen any fresh tracks for bears or cats."

"How far did ya venture in?"

"I didn't." Makwa shook his head. "I found the trail and saw it looked big enough for the wagons, so I marked it on my map. Then I moved on to find other paths."

"Did you find routes to the three camps?" Paul asked.

"Only on the map," Makwa clarified.

"Ah. I see. You did not ride to any camps."

"All were too deep in the forest."

They rode in silence until they reached the trailhead where they'd been forced to turn around the day before. All three men dismounted and studied the ground at the edge of the forest and the area leading in.

"Elk, deer, moose," Makwa said as he discerned the various tracks. "All fresh. Wolves, for certain, and coyotes as well. Just about everything. But what I don't see are signs of bears or cats. Well, at least not yet."

Paul peered down the trail and listened to the world around them, bright and lively as ever nature was. Songbirds, small critters, insects, and snakes all moving through trees and the undergrowth. But it had also been that way yesterday before they'd entered the forest, hadn't it?

There wasn't any use in wondering. It was time to move. Paul and his crew had a job to do and money to make.

"Okay, men. *Allons-y.*"

As it had the day before, all the sounds of the forest ceased abruptly as soon as their horses crossed single file beneath the spotty canopy of the old-growth forest. The bright sunlight that had warmed their backs on the way in faded now, mostly blocked by the thick, leaf-heavy branches overhead. An icy breeze nipped at their cheeks, and damp, cold air clung to their exposed skin, settling quickly into their clothes.

Bébé tensed under the saddle and tossed her head. Paul glanced behind to find the other two horses just as skittish as his own. Most disconcerting to Paul was Bébé's nervousness. The big mare was the bravest horse he'd ever known, especially among the giant breeds and their crosses. The horses all blew hard breaths through their nostrils, snorting their uneasiness.

The gentle whisper of the wind through the trees' giant, thick leaves was the only sound to break the eerie silence.

"*Calme,*" Paul said soothingly to his mare. Makwa and Jack followed his lead, speaking in low, gentle tones until their horses had settled down enough to continue forward. Even though their mounts were nervous, it was safer for the three men to travel on horseback rather than by wagon.

They maintained an easy walk as they moved down the trail. Makwa studied the ground, Paul the trees, and Jack kept his head on a swivel. The game trail, wide at first, became increasingly narrow as it skirted swaths of dead fall. Giant virgin stands of hardwood and white pine trees towered nearby, and the isolated patches of underbrush at their bases seemed to stand sentinel, guarding their masters with thorns, thistles, and crawling spiders.

"What coulda caused this?" Jack asked in a whisper.

"Storms," Makwa answered before Paul could. "Or…"

"Or what?"

"Nothing." He rolled his shoulders back, then stretched his neck to either side. "Just storms."

"Aye. If you say so, Mak."

"Makwa," the man corrected.

Jack's silence was affirmation enough that he'd gotten the message.

The trail progressed into a section of recent growth where a fire must have burned down an area of ancient trees. Brush and saplings and ten- to fifteen-year-old trees grew thick here.

Paul tugged the reins to halt Bébé, studied the position of the sun in the sky, then pulled out his map. They were heading in the right direction. Makwa was right to trust the maps regarding the three camp locations. If the map was right, then they could scout the first camp and cut the trail for the wagons on their way back. It could take a day or two, but it was work that needed to be done.

Farther along, they dismounted the horses to lead them through a strangling patch of underbrush. There was no way around it if they wanted to stick to the game trail that conveniently headed toward the first X-marked location on the map. Paul couldn't help but wonder why the boss had been so specific about that location. Or why Jack had insisted on coming that morning instead of staying near the women and their excellent cooking.

Onyx Eyes

THOUGH IT COULDN'T BE later than mid-morning, the light filtering through the canopy felt more akin to dusk in Paul's mind. Worse, the cool air didn't warm as the day went on, and he pulled his black wool jacket tightly around him. He hadn't brought a scarf with him, not expecting such a creeping cold that made his bones ache. It felt frigid enough that he could have seen his breath puff in the air before him, but it never did. He was worrying he'd come down with a fever, and he'd need to head to the nearest town for a doctor.

Before he could worry himself over whether he had any symptoms of an illness that would keep him from his work, he suddenly broke through the underbrush, and all three men and their horses filed out into a large, dome-like clearing before halting abruptly and taking in the change of scenery. The trees surrounded them in an uncanny perfect circle, their branches intermingling overhead with only a small hole through which the sunlight bore down. Mushrooms sprang up at the edges of the moss, matching the perfect circle of the tree line. A small, crystal-clear stream split the clearing, meandering in small bends from west to east. Paul wasn't much for identifying wild fungi, but even if he had been tempted to try, he wouldn't have dared pluck a single one from its place.

According to the map he'd studied and burned into his brain, the first X marking the intended campsites should have been...here.

The air was warm here, and he relaxed in the relief of it compared to the cold from which they'd come. It smelled of earth and water, clean and undisturbed. His stomach growled with a hunger he hadn't noticed before, and it surprised him since his breakfast had been a hearty meal.

Paul glanced briefly at Makwa and Jack, then turned back and caught his breath as a flurry of color swelled up before him. Orange and black butterflies lifted off the soft blanket of moss covering the floor of the clearing and filled the air. The swift-flowing stream that cut directly through the middle of the clearing wasn't a large body of water, but it wasn't small enough to jump across either.

The flood of monarchs seemed to part ahead of the men as they trudged forward, awestruck, toward the stream. Paul raised a hand to gesture at the perfect circle of the tree line until a butterfly alighted on the very tip of his index finger. He turned it slowly, admiring the beauty of its paper-thin wings, its delicate black antennae, and its tiny fuzzy face set with shiny black eyes. A complex and yet incredibly fragile creature, a true work of the divine.

"What is this place?" Jack asked, his voice so low Paul barely heard him.

He watched Jack's reins fall as he stumbled forward and reached out a hand into the whirling storm of wings. A butterfly landed on his open palm, quickly followed by another on his pinky finger, and a disbelieving, joyful laugh escaped him.

"This..." Makwa answered Jack's question in a hissing whisper, his words trailing off as he joined them farther into the clearing. "This is a sacred place."

"You know of places like this?" Paul asked.

Makwa's eyes glittered with tears, but he shook his head. "My mother told stories of places like this, places where this world's edges blur with the others."

"What others?"

But Makwa didn't answer, too enthralled by the pristine beauty before them and the wild kaleidoscope of butterflies filling the air and covering the earth.

The butterfly on Paul's finger flapped its wings, fluttering away and rising toward the sky. He watched it go until he lost sight of it in the swirling sea of black and orange.

Paul moved toward the stream, eager to slake his sudden thirst. It looked deep enough and cold enough to be full of trout and even salmon if it was connected to the Au Sable. The lure of cold water and fresh fish was too strong to resist, so he surrendered to his curiosity and walked eagerly across the spongy moss, his movements feeling sluggish and blurred as if he'd suddenly stepped into a dream. He spotted the run of giant salmon as he approached, their telltale silver scales flashing through the crystal-clear water as they fought the current from the bright sandy bottom of the creek. "We will have salmon tonight, boys!"

Paul took one more step forward, right to the edge of the bank, and felt his stomach fly into his throat as he plunged through the moss and into the water. Deep and icy, and such an unexpected shock that he didn't even fight or flail; he only barely resisted the urge to inhale. He'd fallen enough in the cold, rushing spring waters of the Au Sable while river driving to know better.

As the cold gripped his bones and his lungs burned, instinct roared to life in Paul's veins. He kicked his feet and pushed with his arms, reaching for the surface. He opened his eyes to find the sunlight glittering above him and knew he only had to push a little harder for just a little longer. With a final, powerful stroke of his long arms and thrust of his legs, he broke the surface and sucked in air.

His vision cleared as he bobbed in the water, and he found faces staring intently at him. But they weren't the familiar faces of Makwa and Jack. These dark faces belonged to strangers, native men and women he had never seen before. They stood along the tree line, staring at him with onyx eyes set in mirthless faces.

Still treading water, Paul turned in a circle to find he was surrounded, and his men were nowhere to be seen. Gray skies thundered a warning above him and the branches overhanging the clearing were barren of all but a few stubborn, dead leaves. All that was green only seconds ago had turned red, orange, and brown.

One man rushed forward and fell to his knees on the bank, studying Paul with emotionless, all-black eyes. The iris and pupil of each eye were pitch black, and so were the whites of the eyes. Those inky orbs seemed to hold the depths of worlds, and Paul felt as if he'd be sucked into them if he couldn't tear his gaze away.

The man shot a hand forward, grabbed Paul by the hair, and plunged his head back into the icy water.

A Sickening, Burning Terror

PAUL FLAILED AND SCRATCHED against the man's hand, clawing and punching wildly to be released before he drowned. The hand and arm were solid, unmoved even by his desperate blows, and for a moment, he feared this was the end. Still punching with every ounce of energy and force he could muster, his chest tightened like a vise. He expelled breath, watching the silvery bubbles rise to the surface without him, and he grit his teeth against the impulse to take a breath.

His hair was suddenly released, but he didn't immediately float upward. More hands grasped at him, taking him by the wrists, and he knew it was another attempt to hold him down in the water. Paul tried to rip himself free, fought with all of his spirit to free himself so he could swim downstream and break the surface for breath.

His lungs were on fire, and his vision blurred, the fight nearly going out of him. The ghostly hands released, slipping away from him. More hands plunged down and clawed into his forearms before hefting him upward.

Paul gasped when he surfaced again and heaved in great breaths of the blessed air, scrambling all the while to get out of the water and away from the bank. But he couldn't see. His vision was obscured, and he panicked, terrified he'd been blinded from being under the water too long.

"Paul!" Makwa shouted. "Let's go!"

"I can't see!" Paul snapped. He grasped the arm that reached out and pulled him farther onto land.

"Wipe your damned eyes," Jack roared beside him. "We have to get the hell out of here!"

Paul swiped at his face, smearing away a heavy layer of black muck from his eyes. They stung when he opened them, but he could see. He stared at the black muck covering his hands and arms and found his entire body was covered in it, from head to toe. Whirling, he studied the spot where he had fallen in the stream.

There was no salmon-filled, crystal-clear stream anymore. Nothing but a tiny, piddling stream flowed along the top of the bog in which they now stood. The green grass and butterflies were gone, and the thick canopy of leaves only beginning to turn for fall was gone, the tree branches now bare.

"Where..." He heaved in breaths as the world spun around him. "Where are—"

A monstrous thud vibrated around them, shaking the earth beneath them and almost taking them off their feet.

Makwa grabbed a handful of Paul's shirt and yanked, dragging him along at a run. He ran half-blind just behind, stumbling and crashing through the dead undergrowth surrounding the clearing. Makwa led them. Both Jack and Makwa were also covered up to their necks in the same black muck. Paul had to blink more of the dripping muck from his stinging eyes so he wouldn't run into one of the giant, ancient trees and knock himself clean out.

As he ran, sounds filtered through to him, half-muffled. The crunching of the leaves beneath their feet, the hushed words of Makwa murmuring something that sounded like a prayer over and over again in his native language.

Paul's side was cramping from the unexpected sprint when behind them came a thunderous crack of branches. Makwa glanced over his shoulder and his eyes widened in horror. Jack stumbled, letting go of Paul's shirt, but caught himself and returned his gaze forward, running faster than Paul had ever seen.

"Don't look back!" he shouted as the distance grew between him and Paul. "Run faster, you fools!"

A sickening, burning terror flooded Paul's skull and poured like liquid down his spine until it permeated every aching muscle in his body. He could swear he felt the hot breath of something on his back and the ground vibrating behind him as he willed his legs to move faster and his strides to be longer. Makwa was now in the lead. Paul was gaining on Silver Jack, and the monster chasing them thundered only steps behind.

A chuff sounded behind them as they burst out of the tree line of the dark, untouched forest and into the bright open skies of the clear-cut land from which they had entered. Makwa spun first, looking toward the trees, his deep brown eyes bulging as he stared at where they'd come out. He grabbed Jack and Paul each by a shoulder before they could pass him, spinning them around so they could bear witness.

There, at the edge of the trees from which they'd just burst, stood the biggest black bear Paul had ever seen. Scars covered its coarse black coat, and its thick yellow fangs were bigger than any of Paul's long, fat fingers. The creature lifted itself, the claws on its gigantic paws twice as long as its fangs. It opened its maw, pointed its snout to the sky, and let out a bone-rattling roar that shook the surrounding trees.

Paul covered his ears and hunched down to keep himself stable, and Jack and Makwa did the same. All three men wavered on their feet as the ground shook, but they managed to stay upright.

Worse even than the sum of all the bear's other parts and its earth-shaking roar were its eyes. Massive, swirling, blood-red pits glowed from the sockets, and Paul felt certain that the creature stared directly at him, hungry and yearning to strip the flesh from his bones.

Its roar trailed off, and it dropped its front paws to the ground. The giant black bear gave three final threatening chuffs before turning and sauntering off into the shadows of the old forest.

"What the hell was that thing?" Jack asked, first to break the silence as they all fought to catch their breaths. He dropped to his ass on the ground. "And don't try to tell me it was just a damn bear."

"It is *not* just a bear," Makwa confirmed as he seated himself on the ground near Jack. Sweat trickled down his face, leaving tracks through a thin layer of black muck.

Paul joined them on the ground. They all faced the forest and the obvious danger that almost had them in its maw. Paul's heart hammered in his chest, and his eyes stung from the sweat and muck clinging to his eyelashes and dripping into his eyes. He studied the tree line and realized something. "The trees..."

"What about them?" Makwa pulled a flask from his satchel and unscrewed the top.

"They still have leaves, and they are still green. In the clearing, after I got out of the water... they didn't." Paul slowly sucked in a deep breath and controlled his exhale, eager to catch his breath and calm his trembling body. "What happened in there?"

"That place is damned!" Silver Jack groaned and eyed Makwa's flask.

"Something *is* wrong," Makwa agreed before passing his flask to Jack. "I only wish I could speak to my elders. But that's at least a week of hard travel."

"And..." Paul looked around, hesitant to be mistaken. "I suppose you do not mean a week on foot."

"No. It'd be twice that, but why—"

"Where are the horses?"

The Deep Shadow of Night

Paul rubbed his hands in a patch of grass to dry the muck, then rubbed them together. Clumps of black filth fell into the dirt beside him.

"We should try calling for the horses before we abandon all hope." Makwa cupped his hands over his mouth and called out. "Kitchi. Kitchi!"

"My canteen is on my horse." Paul reached out toward Jack, who was still holding Makwa's flask.

"All our canteens are with our horses," Jack grumbled and passed the flask to Paul before picking up a rock and hurling it into the trees where the bear had stood only minutes before. "Damn that saloon, damn that fight, and damn you, Paul."

Paul glared at the man. "You mean that?"

Jack said nothing, facing the forest as he hurled another rock into it. He looked ready to open his mouth when something hard hit him in the leg.

"Ahh!" He cried out in pain, clutching his shin. Paul picked up what had bounced off the man's leg. It was the first rock Jack had thrown.

"Watch out!" Paul shouted, but Jack was still reeling from the hit, seated and clutching his shin. He was in no position to block or duck the second rock.

Paul shoved Jack's shoulder in that split second, forcing the big man onto his side in the dirt with a heavy thud.

The rock missed Jack by a finger's width and continued through the air until it landed with a sharp crack against the ground behind them.

Paul shuddered as he imagined what Jack's face would have looked like if the rock had struck home. The giant grump wouldn't have seen the inside of a saloon ever again.

"Holy shit!" Jack pushed himself upright, eyes glistening as he surveyed the two rocks that had been hurled at him. They were both the ones he had thrown into the trees. "Is someone there?"

"If anyone is there, Jack, they will not answer. Perhaps don't throw stones into the forest anymore, eh?"

"Right," Jack agreed, running a hand through his raven black hair.

Paul sat quietly as he peered into the forest, watching for any movement, and chewed on his thoughts.

Makwa whistled for the horses next, but Paul didn't hold his breath waiting for them to come. Instead, he mentally thumbed through all the stories he could remember that the old timers had shared. The ol' fellers who'd been among the first to cut the virgin stands of white pine in this region. Some had shared tales of giant beasts, creatures left over from a time so far in the past that no one could number the years.

And there were the stories missionaries, fur traders, and settlers had heard from the natives when they weren't fighting them. Some reckoned the stories were true, others nonsense, and still others said they were childish ghost stories meant to scare off the white men. That latter bunch insisted the natives would never share all the truth of the legends and beliefs with the invaders, leaving nothing more of their culture to be despoiled and ruined.

Whatever the veracity of the old stories, Paul had a niggling feeling that there was at least a hint of truth in them.

"We need to head back to camp," he said, standing up. "And we must clean ourselves before we arrive."

"What about the horses?" Makwa asked, worry heavy in his voice.

"Have you looked at the sky, Makwa?"

Makwa tipped his head back and studied the sky, looking east first, then slowly turning west. The sun was already falling toward the horizon.

"No. No, it can't be. It was early morning when we entered. That couldn't have been more than an hour ago." He jumped to his feet and looked back and forth between what they understood as east and west. "We must have gotten turned around in the forest."

"We don't have time for this. Look at the tracks. Three horses with riders, Makwa." Paul pointed toward the trail. "Those are our tracks."

Paul helped Silver Jack get to his feet. Jack limped east down the trail while Paul moved close to Makwa.

"There's a lot of ground to cover, *mon ami*."

Makwa shook his head and hurried after Jack. He and Paul easily caught up to the limping man, and Makwa grabbed a stick for Jack to use as a crutch.

They were all in a shockingly disgusting state and returning to camp covered in black muck would worry the crew. That wouldn't be good for their mission to survey the area expected for cutting come November, which was crucial to all of them. Not only was it about the pay now, but about a spot on all future contracts with Langley Lumber or any other logging company that might come through. For most of them, immigrants and people of color, this was the best-paying work they could get, and it usually meant the difference between starving or thriving, between dying young and alone or starting a family and having their own homestead someday.

If they burned a bridge with this logging company, they automatically burned bridges with them all. Word would get around that they'd botched a job, and it wouldn't merely cost the livelihoods of the fourteen people in his party, it would also mean a season without well-prepared work for the hundred men expected to be fellin' in this forest come winter. If they weren't paid well for a full season of cutting, then their families couldn't be paid well. And almost all the businesses in the lumber towns lived and died on the wages of the jacks.

All that to say, a hell of a lot of people's lives were affected by whether Paul and his crew successfully completed the survey. Keeping up appearances that everything was okay was crucial to good morale and to maintaining the crew's confidence in their land-looker.

By the time they reached an area along the trail with a bend in the stream that jutted outward from the dark forest, it was almost too dark to see. The last vestiges of sunlight warmed the western sky to a light purple, but everything east of it was a glittering blanket of darkest blue under an invisible new moon that still lay somewhere beyond the horizon.

"We will stop here for the night," Paul announced softly. Something about the quiet of night, with its symphony of crickets and the occasional input of owls, compelled respect and gentleness of sound. Especially after the bizarre day they'd barely lived through. "In the morning, we will make ourselves decent before returning to camp. When they ask what happened—"

A splashing sound interrupted him, and he froze, along with Jack and Makwa. The splashing continued toward them from the creek, and Paul had the inclination to run, but he didn't want to panic and end up fleeing from a fish or startled deer. But the more he listened, the more he was sure that whatever was in the water was much larger than a fish and better suited to land than water.

He'd nearly ordered Makwa and Jack to back away quietly before running when a horse snorted, blowing air hard through its nostrils. It was just as surprised and nervous as they were. Paul could barely make out the shape of the equine in the near-total darkness.

"Kitchi?" Makwa walked past Paul and reached out a hand, which the horse gently nuzzled. He spoke soothingly to the horse in Ojibwe.

"Do you think the others are here?" Jack said hopefully, though he stayed rooted to where he stood just behind Paul.

"We can only hope." Paul tried to look around, but starlight alone was not enough to break through the deep shadow of night that enveloped the land.

"Let's see," Makwa said. There was a shuffling sound and squeaks of leather and metal. Then a match flared, and a lantern illuminated the area. The glow was soft at first, brightening harshly as Makwa turned the knob to raise the wick.

Paul averted his aching eyes. Then, shielding his face in shadow with one hand, he looked around. Only a few feet away, Bébé and Jack's Belgian slept in the grass, their heads upright, and their legs folded toward their bellies. He breathed a sigh of relief and resisted the urge to run to the horses. Instead, he walked calmly and spoke in low tones to avoid spooking them. He didn't want them kicking, biting, or worse, bolting, if they were startled awake.

Each of the horses bobbed their heads, opened their eyes, and gave a soft snort of greeting. The saddles were all intact, and the men retrieved their canteens without incident.

All three gulped water greedily and emptied their canteens in minutes, then refilled them upstream from where they'd found Kitchi wandering. After drinking enough to slake their thirst, they worked together to collect fallen branches and long-dead but dry branches for a fire. They set it between the creek and the horses and had it roaring in a few minutes. It didn't take any arm twisting for Paul to convince the other men that they'd best bathe before trying to sleep. No one wanted to go a minute longer caked in the itchy, dried-on muck from the bog. They searched within the reach of the firelight for the deepest part of the creek, but it was only knee high. The trio sat naked in the water and scrubbed their bodies before scrubbing their clothes, all nervously glancing toward the inky shadows of the forest to the north side of the stream.

The water was cold, already beginning to chill with the onset of autumn, and Paul's teeth chattered as a gentle breeze stirred the air above the water. He scrubbed his muck-caked clothing with a vengeance, but soon it was too cold for any of them to continue. The men bolted out of the creek and wrapped themselves in their bedroll blankets before hanging their wet clothes on tree branches close to the fire. They ended the evening sitting silently by the fire and eating the scant rations they'd brought along from camp. It was a good thing Paul knew to plan for things going awry. Although today's events hadn't even seemed real, let alone something that could be planned for.

Their fire was already dying. The small pile of wood they'd gathered wouldn't be enough to last the night. He didn't want to spend the night in utter darkness. Not after what had happened in the clearing and being chased by that monster of a bear. He suspected the other two weren't keen on a lack of fire either, so he got to work collecting more wood, his wool blanket wrapped around him. Paul didn't bother asking the other two to help; he knew they were too tired to go scrounging.

Besides, Makwa and Silver Jack had saved his life in the clearing.

They could have run and saved their own hides or left him behind to stumble through the forest as bear bait, but they hadn't. Paul figured the least he could do was let them rest while he gathered more firewood.

Thankfully, their horses seemed to be just as exhausted as the men, so they remained on the ground to rest instead of sleeping while standing up, as they often would. Paul sent Jack and Makwa to huddle with their mounts as he collected wood. When he'd done as much as he could and loaded up the fire, he joined them.

Curled up in their bedrolls, each man pressed against his horse's back for warmth. The horses minded little, except for Jack's, but the gelding didn't do more than groan deeply and toss his head a few times before falling back to sleep.

Rest came in dozing flashes of unconsciousness before some sound from the water or the crackling of the fire startled Paul awake. Visions of the monster bear or the faces of the onyx-eyed strangers from the clearing faded in and out behind his closed eyelids, gripping his heart in fear every time they slinked from the shadows.

There Was No Answer

PAUL FINALLY GAVE UP on sleep and opened his eyes to a bloody dawn breaking in the eastern sky. A chill shook his body, and every over-tight muscle ached in protest as he huddled more snugly under his blanket. It wasn't any use. Dew from the humid air had settled on them while they slept, dampening the wool and sapping away warmth. The clothes he'd hung out last night near the fire were still soaked.

He'd been right about the fire needing more wood to get through the night. A clump of still-glowing coals made him thankful he'd done the extra work despite how tired he'd been. Hell, he was still tired now. He felt as though he hadn't slept at all. Hurting with every movement, Paul gritted his teeth and pushed through it, wrapping his thick, scratchy wool blanket around himself to search for a little more wood in the glow of dawn's rosy, ever-brightening light. Once he figured he had enough to get them through the morning, he stoked the hot coals and added more wood until it was blazing again.

With his blanket knotted around his waist, Paul threaded a sturdy stick through his shirt and held it above the fire until it was as close to dry as he could get it. Then he did the same with the rest of his clothes, putting on each warm piece as he determined them to be dry enough to tolerate. The others were still sleeping, so he did the same for them. He thought it might be funny to drop Jack's clothes in the fire and listen to the Irishman curse up a storm, but decided against it. It wouldn't be fair to Makwa's sisters if Jack had to walk into camp naked. And... Jack hadn't let him die.

That point still surprised Paul. How he was still above ground and breathing was beyond his ability to figure.

He turned his thoughts to the plan for the day. He was eager to get back to camp and drop into his tent for some proper rest. His smoky but warm clothes finally broke the chill that had plagued him all night.

Jack woke with a groan. His Belgian swung his head around, but didn't threaten to bite Jack.

Two days ago, Paul might have laughed at this 'friendship' between Jack and the horse based on mutual hatred and grudging need. But he still saw *them* everywhere, watching him silently, melding in and out of the shadows between the trees in the old forest, so nothing was funny right now. The faces of native men and women with bottomless black pits for eyes stared at him from his periphery, sliding into pockets of darkness as soon as he tried to look at them directly.

"*Bon matin*, Jack. Your clothes are ready."

"Damn it all to hell. I had hoped it was all a nightmare and I'd wake up in my tent back at base camp. Did all that shit really happen yesterday?"

"*Je ne sais pas.*"

"Could ya do me a favor and speak English?" Jack snapped, then he stood and let his blanket fall to the grass before stomping off toward the creek.

"*Non,*" Paul said firmly, wishing he'd accidentally lost Jack's clothes in the fire.

"Damn, it's cold!"

Makwa woke while Jack washed himself. "How long have you been up?"

Paul shrugged. "I wanted my clothes. Yours are beside you."

Looking relieved, Makwa grabbed his pants and shirt from the log where Paul had laid them. "*Merci.*"

"I want to go quickly." Paul picked up Jack's clothes and hurled them at Jack as he returned from the creek.

Jack sprinted to catch the lumpy ball of clothing before it hit the ground. "Damn it, Paul! Yer a mean bastard!"

"In town, they say I am a French son of a bitch. Now hurry."

"If getting back to the rest of our people isn't enough motivation on its own, remember that breakfast will be waiting for us, Jack." Makwa smirked, then clicked his tongue at his horse so he could rub her down and tighten the cinch on her saddle.

"That's all I needed to hear, Mak!" Jack hopped into his pants and shirt, then helped put out the fire and clean up the camp before tending to his horse.

They were on the trail quickly, stomachs growling as they imagined the breakfast awaiting them when they returned. The ride back was shorter than expected, and they were all quiet as they urged their still-tired mounts toward camp. Faces still peered now and then from the tree line, voices still whispered under the rustle of leaves. Paul didn't tell the others what he saw and heard, not wanting either man to panic. He wondered if they were keeping quiet, too. It was easier to write himself off as a paranoid loon than to admit to what he had witnessed over the past day.

So he kept his mouth shut and kept their pace even and steady. Because prey fled, and predators chased. Paul was not prey, so he wouldn't hightail it back. He refused to run from whatever these creatures were that watched their every movement. At least for now, anyway.

Within a half hour, they came upon the ruts from their wagons and the horses began whinnying, calling out for their equine fellows.

"Awan! Kimi!" Makwa shouted excitedly as they approached the last bend near camp. "We need breakfast!"

But there was no answer from Makwa's sisters, and no whinnying answer from the camp horses.

Paul's stomach dropped when he glanced up at the pale blue skies. There wasn't a hint of the gray smoke rising from a well-fed campfire. Birds sang and chipmunks chittered all around them, but he couldn't hear a single word from the camp, which was just beyond a copse of recent growth that blocked it from view. No murmur of conversation or hammering of nails while building the cook shack.

He spurred Bébé into a canter and rounded the bend at speed, only to pull her to a sliding halt once his line of sight to the camp was clear.

"No, no, no!"

When Something Needs Shooting

THE CAMP THEY HAD left bustling with people and energy yesterday stood empty.

Blood spattered the sides of the wagons, and drag marks through the dirt in the middle of camp told the story of what had happened here.

Paul's blood turned to ice as he studied the camp.

"No!" Makwa cried, rushing through camp and knocking over what little supplies remained to search for his sisters. "Awan! Kimi!"

Paul dismounted in a daze and searched for signs of life, overturning wooden crates and barrels, and jumping inside the wagons.

"This can't be happening," Makwa said, his voice filled with desperation. "They can't be gone!"

"What in the three hells happened here?!" Jack added as he hopped off the Belgian and joined Paul in his search.

"Looks to me like a raid," Paul said as he kicked at the dead fire and lowered one hand over the center of it. "Cold. Maybe last night, maybe a few hours ago."

The horses snorted, blowing hard through their nostrils, and their eyes rolled up in their heads as they followed their humans into camp, hopeful for grain and hay. Kitchi entered last, flinching every few steps, but she was a loyal mount and would follow Makwa to the ends of the earth so long as she could walk. The gray trembled and dipped her head to blow at the dirt before jerking up again. She whipped her head from side to side as she followed Makwa, ready to flee if danger presented itself.

"There's no one here," Paul said aloud, confirming what they'd all suspected. His fists clenched and his stomach turned as he thought of Thomas, Awan, and Kimi. The younger men, too. All of his men. They were good men who would have helped a stranger in trouble or a woman or child in need.

And he was responsible for every soul he'd left in this camp the morning before. The sticky blood on the wagons and in the dirt was on his hands.

"Thomas," he whispered. The boy was so young, too young to have come out here, and he knew it. But he hadn't the courage to say no to Ruby's beautiful face, not when she asked him so desperately, and especially not when the tears had slipped down her perfect cheeks as she shared the other horrible fate that may have awaited Thomas.

The guilt socked him in the gut like the meanest punch from Silver Jack, only worse because the pain lingered, held tight by his conscience. He whispered, "*Mon Dieu*, please save the boy."

But Paul had always heard that the Lord helped those who helped themselves, so he swallowed his fear and worry, and sought the trail. He found the drag marks again and studied them closely, following them as he sorted out where they led. The marks circled, crossed other drag marks, and then traced a path out of camp.

It led straight north. Into the old growth.

He stopped less than two strides away from the wood line. There was a clear separation between the old and the new, almost as if an invisible wall stood between the two sides.

"There," he whispered, feeling sick when he spotted a tuft of long black hair hanging from a branch. Makwa rushed to his side, his breath catching when he spotted the hair. He hesitated, frozen in place.

Jack joined them. "That's... It's from one of the women, isn't it?"

"*Oui.*"

"What are we going to do?"

"We have to find them!" Makwa spun and headed for one of the wagons.

"Is that what we're going to do?" Jack sputtered.

"It is the right thing to do, no?"

"And how do we know they're even alive?"

"That is not important. The women, the boy, my men. We cannot leave without them."

Makwa returned, a bow strung over his shoulder, an ax hanging from his belt, and his Winchester "Yellow Boy" rifle leaned over his left shoulder. "Are we gonna sit here and talk all day, or are we going to get my sisters back?"

Paul nodded to his friend, but stared at the wood line again, worry nipping the edges of his mind, eroding his confidence. He knew the right thing to do, and he would do it no matter the cost, but he didn't move right away.

A breeze stirred up, caressing his face and fluttering his clothing. It wasn't just the wind; it was a challenge from the forest.

"Do you feel it?"

"That feeling of being watched?" Jack asked, shifting nervously beside Paul. "I'll get my guns."

"You think they left your guns when they took everything else?" Makwa scoffed.

"Not if you have yer bow," Jack said with a smirk. "I knew ya seemed like a smart one, so I tucked them away in that same compartment where ya hid yer bow. If you have yers, then my guns are still there."

"Then why didn't I see them?"

"I guess I'm better at hiding things." Jack laughed as he rounded the back of the wagon where Makwa had disappeared earlier.

Paul raised an eyebrow at Makwa. "He is full of surprises, eh?"

The man didn't respond, only shaking his head.

"No matter. I'm glad you hid it, and now we have it, I think we'll need it."

Jack strutted around the corner of the wagon, two long-barrel revolvers in either hand, muzzles pointed to the sky. "See? Now what did I tell ya?"

Makwa glared at him, jaw snapped shut.

"Where did you get such a good pair of guns?"

Jack hesitated, the joy dimming in his eyes. "Maybe I'll tell ya someday, over a lot of whiskey."

"And why were they hidden in a wagon instead of with you on the trail yesterday?"

"Because I only bring them out when I think somethin' needs shootin'." His blue eyes darkened as he stared back at Paul. It seemed the Silver Jack from the day before was gone, replaced by the mean drunk Paul had only barely beaten in the saloon two weeks ago.

Paul wouldn't be intimidated, and he didn't have time for pissing games. He was the land-looker and the crew boss, regardless of which version of Silver Jack he was dealing with from minute to minute.

He held Jack's gaze, unblinking, his muscles tense and his fists ready to pulverize the brute if he moved wrong just once. "Are you with us, Jack? To find our people? Makwa and me, we will do whatever is necessary."

"Didn't I make it clear already? Of course I'm wit' ya! Let's go already." Silver Jack shook his head, broke eye contact, and stepped closer to the wood line. "Yer the boss, right? Ya can go first."

Paul nodded his agreement, a little tension releasing from his hands and arms. He checked his gear on his horse, the red leather saddlebags, his bedroll, and his double-bit ax. After brushing a thumb against each blade, he slid it into a specially fitted strap to hang from his saddle.

He mounted his horse, and Makwa and Silver Jack followed suit.

"I am the boss," Paul said as he lightly tapped Bébé's sides. "And I do not shy from leading."

As they crossed the invisible border of the wood line, all sounds of forest life faded away. The temperature dropped and the breeze died instantly. Paul fought to hide the shiver that rolled through his body.

Dragging Him Away

ALL WAS QUIET IN the forest. Too quiet.

There was no movement in leaf litter on the forest floor or in the branches of the ancient trees stretching high above them. Birds, if they were there at all, made no sound.

The drag marks led Paul on and off guide trails, north and west. They skirted the rim of a steep, bowl-shaped depression in the forest. Leaves occasionally floated down from the canopy in shades of yellow, red, and brown, joining their fellows waiting below. There should have been serenity in watching the trees shed their colorful leaves ahead of winter, but it reminded Paul of death.

The red reminded him of the blood splatter at camp, and he was on high alert for locks of long black hair. As the trio reached the northern edge of the rim, he spotted a ridge rising farther to the north, and a vision flared to life in his mind.

He halted Bébé and pulled the map of the campsites from his saddlebags. There it was.

The easternmost X-marked spot was located due west of where he now stood. And the drag marks headed straight for it.

Makwa rode up beside him and patted Kitchi's neck as he asked, "What's wrong?"

"Uh," Paul tipped his head toward the site he'd been instructed to build first, "the trail goes west here."

"And? We shouldn't be wasting time, Paul. Let's move faster now!"

Holding up the map, Paul pointed at the depression and then the X. "It is strange, no?"

"What's strange, Paul?" Makwa asked, too worried to bother hiding the frustration in his voice. "State your point."

"The trail leads to the first X on the map. Why would the crew be taken to a place marked on a map that Langley gave to me?"

"I agree," Jack said as he rode up to join them and take a closer look at the map. "It's awfully strange."

The bright metal of the guns now hanging from Jack's hips caught Paul's eye, reflecting filtered sunlight coming through the dancing treetops.

"Strange or not, Makwa is right." Paul returned the map to the saddlebags and paused as he retied the flap. They seemed almost...wet. He lifted his fingers to find them dripping a red-tinted liquid, perhaps the dye seeping out of the fine leather. Quickly, he wiped it on his shirt and took his reins in hand. "We will be ready, but we must hurry."

He turned his horse west and bumped his heels to her sides. She leaped into a canter, and they followed the dark trail, the drag marks scarring the otherwise pristine picture of nature cloaked in autumn beauty.

Paul was wrong. They were not ready.

Nothing could have prepared them for the horror they found when they rounded a cluster of giant trees.

As soon as they entered the clearing, Bébé reared first, followed by Kitchi and Jack's Belgian. Paul reined Bébé in a circle to keep her from falling over backward, then spurred her forward.

"Joseph!"

His fellow French Canadian, the man with whom he'd been looking forward to sharing many conversations in their shared native language, was tied across the flat top of a giant, reddish granite and quartz boulder in the center of the clearing. Blood had seeped down the sides of the massive rock, almost fully coating it. Sunlight reflected off the silvery flecks within and cast patches of darkened red light on the ground immediately surrounding the boulder.

Paul threw himself from the saddle and half-stumbled, half-ran across the perfect spongy moss toward Joseph. Right before he reached his crewman, the wind kicked up in the clearing, sending leaf litter swirling through the air, and a blast of air and leaves knocked him onto his back.

"Paul!"

He recognized Makwa's voice even as he struggled to catch his breath. The blast had knocked the wind out of him.

A hand grabbed his shoulder, and when his vision cleared, he found Makwa dragging him away from the boulder.

"No!" Paul scrambled to his feet. But before he could try to reach Joseph again, Makwa slapped something hard against his chest.

He grabbed at it instinctively. It was his ax. When he looked up again toward Joseph, he froze in place and his jaw fell slack.

Between Paul and the boulder where Joseph lay was a swirling, humanoid form made entirely of red, orange, and brown leaves. Branches extended like horns from its head and glowing red eyes glared at him so intensely he nearly felt their heat boring through him.

"Swing, damn it!" Makwa ducked aside as the creature swiped an elongated, leafy arm at him.

Slower to move, the creature struck Paul instead and delivered three deep gashes from the sharpened sticks that formed claws at the end of its arms. He rolled away over the spongy moss floor of the clearing and sprang up a few feet away. The creature floated toward him, its red eyes seeming to narrow in annoyance as it followed.

The report of a gun thundered through the clearing, and another. Paul watched a couple of leaves flutter in the creature's abdomen as if they'd been disturbed.

The shots hadn't damaged the monster even a little. It snapped its head toward Jack and let out a bone-aching hiss that made the shooter cover his ears and tip out of his saddle. As soon as Jack was on the ground, the creature returned to its pursuit of Paul.

Hoping to lead it away from the clearing and the men, Paul spun toward the tree line, ready to push off into a sprint. He hesitated when he found a wall of trees surrounding the clearing. It formed in a perfect circle, just like the clearing they'd been caught in the day before. The resemblance brought back terror-filled memories, and unknown fear flooded him when he realized there was no way out.

Another blast struck Paul, this time from his right side. It pounded his ribs and sent him hurtling through the air. He hit the ground and tumbled for several feet before stopping. Dizzy, he struggled to his feet, looking for the creature but seeing double. As his vision cleared, he was surprised to find he'd held on tight to the ax.

He gripped the smooth handle tightly as the levitating creature headed his way, leaves and debris rising in its wake.

"I can't get a clear shot," Jack yelled with his pistols readied and aimed at the creature directly between them.

Paul quickly understood the problem. If Jack fired and the bullets passed through the creature, they could hit Paul.

From Paul's right near the boulder, Makwa fired an arrow.

Just as the bullets had, the arrow passed through the thing, barely disturbing the leaves swirling together to make up its body.

The leaf-filled body paused, expanded briefly, then contracted back into its strange form before continuing to pursue him. Paul gritted his teeth, gripped the ax handle in both hands, hefted it over his shoulder, and as it closed the distance between them, swung with all his might.

His ax sliced through the monster from shoulder to hip, sailing through the body and knocking away a handful of sticks and leaves. The creature was split diagonally only for a few seconds before its swirling mass pulled the pieces back together in the humanoid shape.

"Tabernak!"

The creature's glowing red eyes bore down on Paul. It snatched him up by the neck, its pointed stick fingers pressing into his throat as it raised him skyward and glared up at him.

With his airway cut off, Paul dropped his ax and pounded against the creature's arms with his fists. His vision darkened quickly, but he spotted Jack on his Belgian cantering toward them.

Everything went black, and sounds grew muffled.

Paul was vaguely aware of a falling sensation before he hit the ground, but it took what felt like an hour for the return of oxygen to wake his brain again. Light slowly returned to his vision, and he reached out a hand and searched the grass around him for his ax. His fingers found the handle and wrapped around it, pulling it to him as he pushed himself to his knees.

The fuzzy colors dancing in his vision wavered into clarity, and he found Jack lying still on the ground near the boulder, and the creature closing in on Makwa.

The Blood-Soaked Stone

MAKWA STOOD WITH HIS back to the boulder at Joseph's feet, a hatchet in one hand, ready to swing at the monster.

"Makwa!" Paul shouted a warning as he hurled his ax. Makwa heeded just in time and dove toward Jack's still form as the ax hit the creature. The ax knocked out the long sticks that formed the creature's legs before continuing through and striking a bulbous pocket of quartz on the boulder.

Sparks from the ax strike on the quartz showered the creature. Swirling leaves caught fire and flames licked across its swirling body. The creature blasted more wind in its pain and fury, and the oxygen-hungry flames burned hotter and brighter, consuming the body.

Paul heaved in giant breaths as he limped to where Makwa kneeled next to Jack. Together, they watched the creature flail and dart wildly throughout the clearing, scaring the trapped horses. It let loose an ear-piercing screech that echoed and bounced off the surrounding trees, disorienting Paul and Makwa.

Paul barely stayed upright enough to witness its throes, squinting through the pain, determined to keep his eyes on the monster. But as the flames ran out of fuel, the screech faded until nothing was left but ash and echoes.

A small dust devil swirled the ashes of the creature into the air, twisting and rising until the dissipating specks of white and gray disappeared above the trees.

Paul wanted nothing more than to throw himself on the moss so he could catch his breath and rest his body. Instead, he put a hand on Makwa's shoulder, and they nodded in silent agreement that whatever had just happened was over. They turned their attention to Jack.

Makwa whistled for his horse, and it came, though it snorted and trembled nervously. He took his canteen from the saddle, splashed a little water on Jack's face, and gently shook his shoulder. "Jack? Jack!"

Paul looked over his shoulder, wary of any more creatures. Nothing else stirred in the clearing except for the horses, twisting their heads and blowing hard through their nostrils. But Paul did spot something that gave him a breath of relief; the wall of trees had disappeared. The trees were once again naturally spaced, with plenty of room between them, as was usually the case with old growth.

That meant they could leave.

"Makwa." He grasped his friend's arm and nodded toward the tree line. "The path is open again."

Makwa glanced upward, studied the circle of trees, then patted Jack's face. "Come on, we need to leave!"

Paul stood and limped the few strides it took to reach the boulder. He nearly leaned on it for support, then hesitated, thought better of touching the blood-soaked stone. Reaching over carefully, he placed his fingers against Joseph's neck.

Cold. No pulse.

It was exactly as Paul had expected, but he'd still needed to try. What Paul hadn't seen until now were Joseph's guts spilled out all over the forest floor on the opposite side of the boulder.

The man's open eyes stared upward into the cloudless fall sky. Paul closed them. "Do you have any coins, Makwa?"

Makwa fished two from a pocket and tossed them one at a time to Paul, who placed them over Joseph's eyelids.

"*Repose en paix*, Joseph."

Paul considered burying him, but there was no time. It looked to be midday already, and he wanted to find the rest of his crew and keep them from being slaughtered before nightfall overtook the forest.

Jack finally stirred, groaning deeply. "What in the hell happened?"

Makwa looked at Paul, and Paul shrugged. He couldn't fathom how to answer that question fully, so he stuck to the facts.

"That... thing that attacked us is gone. Joseph is," he swallowed hard, "he's dead."

"One of the crew." Jack rubbed at his head. "Was... was there a...a something attacking us? Some wild bunch of... leaves and... wood?"

Paul nodded, then mounted Bébé carefully, his every move painful. He pulled the campsite map from the red saddlebags. Blood came away on his fingers, and he studied it carefully. How had blood gotten on his saddlebags?

He pulled a handkerchief from his shirt pocket and wiped his hands clean, then felt all over his face, head, and body for cuts, scrapes, or anything else that might bleed enough to drip. There were plenty of cuts and scrapes, but none of them were still bleeding. Even the triple parallel gashes on his arm had stopped actively bleeding. After wiping his hands once more, he rubbed his thumb against the flap of his right saddlebag.

It came away smeared with blood again.

"Am I going mad?!"

Makwa helped Jack onto the Belgian, then mounted his own horse. "At this point, I think we all are."

"I think... no. It is ridiculous." Paul simply couldn't deal with the question right now. And he didn't need to add anything else that might make his men want to hightail it out of here. They were up against...

He hadn't the first idea what they were up against. This was nothing like what he had seen during his first season. And where was the rest of his crew? Paul needed Makwa and Jack's help to find them and keep them from Joseph's fate.

Makwa wouldn't be going anywhere without his sisters, but Jack might be tempted to flee. And after whatever injury he'd sustained after charging the creature from horseback, maybe it was the right thing to do. After all, the man had saved Paul's life twice now.

"Jack," Paul started.

"I ain't goin' nowhere, ya French son of a bitch."

"Well, then, I have more strange news." He held up the map so the other two could see and pointed at the easternmost X on the map. "We are here."

Neither man answered.

Jack blinked and shook his head. "And yer point is?"

"This place was marked on my map as the first site where Monsieur Langley wanted us to build a camp for the coming season."

"Wait. Are you sure?" Makwa gestured around the clearing. "The ground is too soft here. It's almost a bog, and it would likely flood with a mild winter or an early spring rain."

"I see that too," Paul agreed. "Langley told me these were scouted by the camp who cut the forties south of here last winter. No lumber boss or seasoned jack would pick this spot for a camp."

"Then what do ya think happened?" Jack held one palm to the side of his head over a welt.

Paul shrugged. "I do not know. But I would bet my pay that any tracks leading from here will go to the next camp. We must pray that we can find them there."

"And if not? What's after that?" Makwa asked before looking around the clearing to study tracks.

"After that? There is a third campsite. But..."

"Don't be holding back on me now, Paul." Jack urged his horse closer to Paul. "We've been through hell already. Just tell me."

Paul sighed. "The third site is where I fell in the bog yesterday."

Let Us Harvest

PAUL DIDN'T LOSE HIS bet. After identifying exactly where the three of them had entered the clearing, they found a trail leading out the western side. The tracks of eight horses, likely carrying riders, and more than a dozen people on foot led out of the clearing on a north-westerly route.

Paul, Makwa, and Jack rode the ten miles hard as the sky grew dark and heavy with rain clouds. They rode fast, following the trail left by the group ahead of them. It took longer than Paul had hoped, and by the time they reached the second campsite, thunder rumbled a soft warning far in the west.

As they closed in, dead and fallen trees became more regular. Pits and mounds, common to the old-growth forests, were overwhelming here. An overabundance of dead fall pitted and pocked the landscape, and trees leaned and crossed over each other everywhere. Fewer stand-ing trees meant a sparser canopy, and it dampened Paul's spirit. Not only was it yet another oddity, but without the canopy, they'd be entirely at the mercy of the storm heading their way.

On hearing chants rising through the trees, they halted and dis-mounted, loosely tying their horses' reins to the overturned roots of a fallen giant white pine. When the men huddled together between Bébé and the Belgian, Paul said, "I don't know what is happening, but I feel we need to move quickly."

"Agreed," Makwa said, readying his rifle. His bow was slung over his shoulder. "Let me lead the way. You two follow my path exactly."

"Ready." Jack grinned and lightly rattled the pistols he held muzzle-up in each hand. Paul could only pray that Jack was good enough with those guns to avoid hitting their crew with bullets or ricochets from the boulder.

Makwa led them on a route around the tree-encircled clearing that offered the most coverage for an approach from the north. This meant they avoided taking the same path as the group they'd tracked and, hopefully, would evade an ambush. The trees around this clearing were all dead, burned to black char at their pointed tops, as if lightning had struck each, severing them halfway. All around the circle of burnt boles, every tree for at least twenty feet had fallen, landing with its top pointing outward.

The incoming storm blew frigid gusts of wind through the forest. When Makwa reached a spot near the clearing concealed by a wall of tangled tree roots covered in clumps of dried earth, he gestured for them to stop.

At the foot of a single boulder of melded jasper and quartzite, Paul spotted a group of people kneeling with their hands tied behind their backs. They were his people. Lars was among them, and so was Kimi. Two faces he didn't see kneeling among the rest were Awan and Thomas. From his current position, he could see the area immediately around the boulder, and counted six men in trail coats and hats surrounding his people. Some held rifles, others pistols.

He turned to his own men and found Makwa wearing a pained expression, his brows deeply furrowed. Paul caught his attention, then shook his head slowly, warning his friend against acting on impulse. After swallowing hard, Makwa nodded once. They both returned their attention to the clearing.

Paul couldn't identify the language of the chant, though it sounded vaguely familiar. He waved at Makwa and Jack and cupped a hand over one ear to ask if they understood it, but both shook their heads. As they watched, three men shrouded in black cloaks approached the kneeling members of Paul's crew and raised their arms, palms facing up. The volume of their repeated chanting rose as they stretched their arms to the sides. A sharp gust of wind blasted through the clearing, whipping up fallen leaves and light debris. When an ear-piercing screech resounded above them and broke the chant, Paul pressed his hands over his ears and looked skyward.

Giant, black-feathered wings beat rhythmically high above the clearing as an enormous bird circled in the upper air stream. The beast screeched again, then tipped its sleek, narrow head down, brought its wings close to its body, and dove toward the clearing with its talons outstretched. The body of the huge raptor entered the clearing and proved surprisingly agile as it swooped up at the last minute to alight on the ground next to the boulder.

The beast stood higher than two men, and Paul guessed its wingspan to be at least thirty feet. Cocking its head, blood-red eyes the size of turkey platters surveyed the gathered humans. A white crown of delicate feathers sat like a wreath around the back of its head, and they bounced with every movement.

"Animikii!" Makwa hissed.

"What?" Paul asked, careful to keep his voice from traveling beyond the tree roots that shielded them.

"It's a thunderbird!"

The chanting that had paused when the bird entered the clearing started again, but this time, it switched to another language. The chant was shorter now, but in a language Paul recognized: Latin. Familiar from a childhood spent at Mass.

Roughly, he translated the chant in a whisper for Makwa and Jack.

"We offer blood to the old gods, the gods of shadow and light, that they let us harvest the bounty of the forest."

"What in the hell?" Jack whispered, shaking his head.

"I don't like the sound of that." Makwa readied his rifle. "Animikii is supposed to protect human life. Why would these men offer blood?"

The thunderbird lifted one leg and used its talons to snatch one of Paul's crewmen from where he knelt between the bird and the boulder. Paul immediately recognized the Norwegian man as Anders, a jack who'd been with the company for four years now. Anders struggled against the rib-breaking squeeze of the thunderbird's grip, pounding his fists against the beast's feet as it raised him up.

But it was no use.

The thunderbird opened its long, sharp black beak and plucked Anders's head off in one swift action, taking part of the spinal column with it. Gore sprayed over the people gathered, some gasping out and others crying in terror.

Paul's first urge was to shout out and rush the beast, but Anders was gone. There was no human way to repair the damage done, to save him. He was too stunned to utter any noise, too sick to risk opening his mouth. Makwa and Jack were just as silent and frozen beside him. They watched together in utter horror as the beast lifted its beak, and the man's skull and attached spinal column slid down its gullet.

The trio of would-be heroes weren't the only ones struck frozen in terror. Paul's crew, the three cloaked men, and their hired guns all stared at the bird. No one moved a muscle or made a sound again until the bird tossed the rest of Anders's body against the boulder. It hit the spot where the jasper met the quartz with a sick thud and left a bloody trail down the side of the boulder as it dropped on top of the kneeling people. Kimi screamed, and two men cried out as the twitching, blood-spurting body pushed them face down into the dirt. She squirmed until she could wiggle herself free.

With a sharp squawk, the thunderbird turned its head and stared down at Kimi, then shuffled closer toward her.

"No, no! Please don't do this," Kimi begged, sobbing.

Just as it reached its black talons toward the hopeless young woman, the thundering report of Makwa's rifle rang out. Paul, too close when Makwa fired, felt a deafening pain. Now all he could hear was a high-pitched ringing above the muffled noises around him. He didn't let that stop him. Paul rounded the tree roots with his double-bit ax raised. Jack ran around the other side, both his revolvers bucking in his hands as he fired shot after shot at the thunderbird.

Together, they stormed into the clearing.

He Raised His Ax

THE BURST OF GUNFIRE startled the thunderbird, and it hopped back, opening its wings and flapping to steady itself. Red eyes blinked rapidly before the beak opened to let out an angry screech at Jack and Makwa. Bullet impacts peppered the massive feathers over the bird's wings and body, but they seemed to do little damage.

That didn't matter to Makwa. He ran howling toward the beast, racking the lever after every shot fired to automatically load the next round. By the time they reached a point between the thunderbird and the kneeling crew near the boulder, Makwa had fired five of his fifteen rounds, and Silver Jack, having emptied both revolvers, bolted behind the jasper end to reload.

Paul had run into the clearing last and now found himself on a straight path toward the chanting men. Their faces were shrouded in shadow under the hoods of their cloaks, but from what he could see of their mouths, they were more shocked by the appearance of Makwa, Jack, and Paul than they were by the descent of the thunderbird.

Raising his ax over one shoulder with both hands, Paul was almost in striking range of the nearest one when a thick man in a dark brown duster intercepted him with a rifle butt to the face.

He went down fast, dazed as bright spots filled his vision, but Paul somehow willed himself to roll aside. He was seconds from death when a shotgun blast exploded in the spot where he'd fallen.

"No!" a man shouted with authority. "Don't shoot him!"

After a hard shake to clear his vision, Paul pushed himself to his feet. The man who'd struck him now strode toward Paul with his shotgun in both hands, clearly ready to deliver another cranium-splitting buttstroke to the head. Paul spotted his ax. He'd dropped it on the ground when he took the hit, but it was behind the gunhand coming for him now.

Paul took the risk, diving forward and rolling under the swing of the shotgun. He came out of the roll just within reach of his ax and wrapped his fingers around the handle. Using the momentum of a spin as he pushed off his toes, he swung the ax in a backhand motion as hard as he could as he leaped upward toward the gunhand.

The ax blade sliced through the gunhand's wide-brimmed black hat and slammed halfway through his skull, dropping him like a sack of potatoes. Paul placed one boot against the gunhand's chest and ripped the ax out with a spray of gore.

He turned again and, in a split second, hurled the ax at one of the gunhands, who was raising his shotgun. It struck the man in the shoulder and severed his arm clean through. The man stared in shock as his arm spun away from him. His shotgun dropped to the ground butt-first, discharging on impact and blasting a third gunhand in the chest. He toppled backward and slammed into the ground.

Paul was on his way to finish the job on the one-armed man when a bolt of lightning exploded through the air next to his head. He ducked away, lost his footing, and fell to the ground. Scrambling, he found his ax in the low light just as the first few raindrops splashed into his messy hair. Once he turned to survey the situation, the rain began to pour, turning the clearing into a pit of blood-soaked muck. Overhead, the light gray skies had turned dark and menacing, with roiling thunderheads massing together and swirling in place. Blue and white lightning arced through the air between the clouds and the thunderbird, sending the bolts through the clearing in chaotic and random spurts. The bolts danced across the bird's feathers and down its body, harmless to the nightmarish creature.

Makwa exchanged his rifle with his bow, an arrow nocked and aimed at the thunderbird. Jack slunk around the boulder, and before Paul could worry, he watched one of his crew go free and head toward the horses while Jack crouched next to another kneeling person.

Paul stood over the one-armed man and hefted his ax in both hands, holding it high and hesitating. He should have simply swung it down and ended the man quickly. But he didn't see just a gunhand anymore. He saw a shocked boy, confused and terrified, no more than nineteen years old. And that young man's life was now in Paul's hands. Something about him reminded Paul of himself all those years ago in that first season. Alone in the woods and seeing things no one would ever believe.

Lowering the ax, Paul stared into the boy's eyes for a brief moment. He looked around for the other gunhands, but he couldn't see to the western side of the clearing where he thought he'd spotted the cloaked men running. So he left the boy and sprinted to join Makwa, who was evading the talon swipes of the thunderbird and fighting the gusts thrown by its massive black wings. As Paul reached Makwa's side, he raised his ax to meet the bird's beak as it snapped at his best friend.

Makwa slammed into Paul's side with his shoulder and sent him stumbling, and the ax missed by over a foot.

Furious as he regained his balance, Paul shouted at Makwa, "Why? I could have stopped this!"

Makwa fired an arrow, and Paul watched as it barely grazed the side of the creature's body. The thunderbird was too close to miss; it was like aiming and firing at the broad side of a barn. Paul knew Makwa was an excellent marksman and archer; he shouldn't have missed. But he nocked an arrow, and again only grazed the creature's side, the arrow merely caressing its feathers.

"Get them out of here!" Makwa tipped his head toward the crewmen still bound and kneeling in front of the boulder.

This creature must have been very special to Makwa if he was willing to defend it, even after it had viciously killed Anders and had nearly done the same to his little sister. So Paul did as he was asked and headed toward the boulders. He kept low to the ground, hoping it would reduce his chances of getting struck by the arcing lightning bolts.

"Help me cut them free," Jack shouted above the driving rain just as a crack of thunder made them all duck.

Paul cast a worried glance Makwa's way, but he was too fast for the bird, ducking and rolling away when the talons swiped or the beak snapped at him. Joining Silver Jack, Paul slid his Sheffield Bowie from its sheath and made quick work of cutting his crew members free. The pair alternately watched Makwa dodge the bird's attacks and kept an eye out in case the chanting men sent their hired guns in to attack again.

But when Paul rounded the thunderbird, he caught a glimpse of the men in his periphery. They watched silently from the other side of the clearing while sitting atop their horses. The three remaining gunhands all rode as well. Something looked odd about their saddles and bedrolls, but Paul could barely make out what he was seeing through the downpour. Visibility was simply too poor. But the men only watched as Makwa kept the bird diverted and Paul and Jack freed the crew.

With Jack's help, they lifted Anders's body off the trapped crew members and freed them. As each person was cut free, Paul and Jack sent them north toward the horses.

When the last of the crew disappeared out of the clearing, Paul shouted to Makwa. "Get away from it! They are free!"

Makwa waved his left hand at Paul, then slung his bow over his shoulder and waved both arms at the creature. He shouted something at the thunderbird in Ojibwe, and Paul felt the heaviness of words he couldn't understand weigh on his heart. The bird froze, a black-taloned foot halting mid-swipe.

The lightning dancing across the feathers of the thunderbird slowed as the bird cocked his head to stare at Makwa, leaning down close. It studied him with those blood-red eyes as Makwa held both hands palm up to the creature and dropped to his knees in the mud, moss, and water. Makwa bowed his head, and Paul's heart leapt into his throat.

Paul wanted to scream, rush out to save the only man he'd ever known as a true friend, but something deeper told him to stay put and keep his mouth shut. This was not his moment; it was Makwa's.

The dancing lightning dissipated as the bird lifted a giant, black-feathered wing and rested it gently around Makwa's body. As the creature trilled softly—almost as if speaking to Makwa alone—it emanated a pulsing blue glow. Then the thunderbird retracted its wing, screeched one final time, and launched itself straight into the sky.

Tears filled Makwa's eyes as he watched the bird disappear into the dark clouds, carrying the storm away as it headed east. Emotions pinched Paul's chest and tightened in his throat. His eyes burned, threatening tears. He didn't understand what he'd just witnessed, but it felt spiritual. It reminded him of the stories his native grandmother had told him.

The thundering of horses' hooves snapped him from his memories, and he spun toward the sound to find the three cloaked men and their three gunhands galloping out of the clearing. On the backs of two of the gunhands' horses lay sights that turned Paul's stomach—a slender adult body tied face-down behind one man, and a child-sized body tied behind another.

A Future He Could Not See

PAUL HURLED HIS AX at the last rider—one without a body laid over the butt of his horse—hoping to kill him and knock him out of his saddle so he could steal his mount. But the ax missed the gunhand's head by a hand's breadth, lodging into a tree at the edge of the clearing.

"Damn it!" Paul roared into the sky, white-knuckled fists stretched out to his sides as he raged at his failure.

Even Jack jumped a little, staring at him with wide eyes, his hands hovering near the Colts slung at his hips.

Makwa jumped to his feet and raced toward the edge of the clearing, but Jack stopped him short.

"They were all on horseback. We need to ride, too, or we'll never catch up."

"Awan?" Makwa asked, the lines around his eyes furrowed deep with worry.

"They have her and Thomas," Paul said with a growl. He put his thumb and his forefinger to his mouth and whistled. For a moment, nothing happened. Then Bébé's blue roan body came crashing through the wood line, and she bounded into the clearing, making a beeline for Paul. He didn't flinch as she cantered toward him; he merely stepped to the side as she slid to a stop within inches of him, threw the dangling reins over her head, and flung himself up into the saddle. She snorted and spun in a circle when he picked up the reins.

"Paul, wait," Silver Jack started, marching toward him. "I think we need to—"

"Makwa," Paul interrupted, "I'll go after Awan and Thomas. Take the rest of our crew south out of the forest and get them somewhere safe."

"No," Makwa said, shaking his head. "You're not going alone. That's my sister—"

"And Kimi is your sister, too. Take her, take our men, and trust me to handle this. Jack, you help them get to safety, *s'il te plaît*." Paul tipped his head skyward. The storm clouds were gone now, but the sky was orange with the setting of the sun. "It will be dark soon, and there is even more danger to fear in this place when the night falls."

With that, Paul bumped the heels of his boots into Bébé's sides, and she leaped forward into a canter. They headed out the same way the cloaked men and the gunhands had disappeared. Paul halted just long enough to wrench his favorite ax out of the dead white pine he'd struck instead of the gunhand he'd been aiming for.

Men yelled out for him, but instead of stopping and turning to hear them out, Paul stood in his stirrups and held his ax aloft in a farewell salute.

He didn't have the luxury of time to discuss things; he knew what needed to be done.

Daylight was fading fast, and if he couldn't reach the third site before it was completely dark, he risked losing the trail and wandering lost in the pitch-black forest. That thought was more frightening than anything else his mind could conjure up.

He focused on his mission rather than his fears, keeping his seat as Bébé burst through bushes and jumped over fallen branches, ducking when the deadfall was high enough to trot under. She seemed to know where she was going, perhaps by picking up on the scents of the other horses. From what he could tell by their direction and his memory of the map, they were on a direct path to the clearing with the stream that he'd found the day before. The thought of the place threatened to send shivers through his body, but he kept control of his mind and pushed the feelings back.

The silence of the darkening forest didn't help matters, so he delved into his memory of the clearing, the perfectly circular ring of trees and mushrooms, its entirely moss-covered floor, and the crystal-clear stream that split the area nearly perfectly.

Shadows became thicker as the sun fell lower in the sky and the well-spaced old-growth trees gave way to more dead fall and new-growth spots full of saplings, young fruit trees, and berry bushes. Paul grew nervous as they slowed, and it became a struggle to make out the tracks they'd been following. He wanted to trust the mare to follow the trail, but she was a horse, not a hound, and he needed to be absolutely sure they were on the right path.

Then he heard it, just as he had before: chanting in a language he didn't understand and couldn't identify. His muscles tensed and his stomach tightened with anxiety as he pulled Bébé to a halt. He looped the knot in the reins over the saddle horn. It kept her reins loose but up where she wouldn't get tangled in them and hurt herself.

As quietly as he could, Paul dismounted, sliding from the saddle instead of using the stirrups so the leather wouldn't creak as much. The soft ground muffled the sound of his feet hitting the forest floor and, luckily, he hadn't landed on any sticks. He stroked Bébé's neck and whispered in her ear, *"Reste ici, s'il te plaît."*

He couldn't shake the sensation that he was saying goodbye, and he couldn't bear the thought of anything happening to the stout mare. She was the most loyal creature he'd ever known, even among the humans. But Paul had no more time to worry about a future he could not see.

He pulled his ax from its strap on his saddle, gave Bébé one last pat, then crept through the undergrowth toward the edge of the clearing.

Striking Distance

Two horses strained at their load on the north side of the stream. Their haunches ducked as they fought to move forward, straining against harness lines that were tied to something under the water's surface. From the way the lines were spaced, Paul figured it had to be something massive. The horses' ears were pinned back as they listened to the gunhand's shouts urging them to haul up their load. Long harness reins led from the horses down into the stream. At least it wasn't currently the muck-filled bog he'd crawled out of yesterday.

"Hup, hup!" the gunhand shouted gruffly. This one looked tougher than the rest, with a nasty scar running down his cheek and small scars criss-crossing his hands. The other two gunhands stood behind the horses, helping to pull at the harness lines. Their clothing was dripping wet, and their breaths puffed in the chill air as they slipped on the soft moss and fought to help pull something from the water. They'd be a little less dangerous as the early cold sapped away their energy.

Several standing torches ringed the clearing, casting a dancing orange glow throughout the area. Three lanterns rested on the ground near the cloaked men whose chanting hadn't ceased despite the work of the gunhands, their flames glowing calmly. The men stood in a circle, and between them lay two still forms.

Paul's throat tightened and his mouth went dry. His hands wrung painfully around the ax. He'd never crossed the stream along the way and therefore found himself on the north side as well, making it a hell of a lot easier to rush them. He was ready to raise his ax and charge when the lead gunhand gave a final whoop and holler as he drove the horses away from the stream and something huge rose out of the water and was dragged onto the bank.

It was a gigantic chunk of copper. Just like the other clearings, this one had a boulder too, only it had been submerged, hidden in the stream. It was smaller than the previous boulders but still easily the size of two horses, and it likely weighed ten times as much. The massive chunk of copper gleamed in the torch and lantern light, hypnotizing Paul. He knew copper well and had seen small chunks and flakes of gold and silver in this region too. But there was no mistaking copper. It was even blotched with small spots of blue-green oxidization in various rough pits along the surface.

The gunhands unhooked the horses and tied them to trees at the northern edge of the clearing where the rest of the mounts had been left. Meanwhile, the lead gunhand strode over to the circle of cloaked men and bent down to pick up Awan first, positioning her gently over one shoulder before depositing her body on the copper boulder. He returned and did the same with Thomas.

It struck fear into Paul's heart to see them unmoving. He didn't understand what could have rendered them unconscious for so long without killing them.

Once the gunhand had positioned Thomas on the boulder next to Awan, the cloaked men continued their chanting, but moved to surround the boulder. Unlike in the last clearing, nothing happened right away. There was no gust of wind, stirring of leaves, or strange magick filling the place. The absence of the feeling surprised Paul, considering all that he'd witnessed today, and how strangely things had gone sideways in this very place only the day before.

But he didn't want to wait until things got wild. It would be hard enough to safely rescue an unconscious Awan and Thomas from the gunhands and their tough-looking leader without adding any more monstrous creatures of legend to the mix.

Especially since he'd be alone this time.

Paul watched as the chanting faded without switching to Latin as it had before, and one of the cloaked men pulled out a long, ornate dagger and held it high. That steeled Paul into action. He gripped his ax, mentally reviewed his path out of the wood line, and counted the strides between the gunhands and the cloaked men. Then he burst into the clearing, both hands gripping his ax overhead, and used all his height and power to rush the man with the dagger. He was in striking distance within seconds, and his ax arced down on the dagger-wielding man's cloaked head.

But the tough with the scar was faster. The leader of the gunhands shoved one of the soaking wet gunhands in front of the ax blade, and it was too late for Paul to stop his swing, even if he'd wanted to. Anyone who stood between him and the two people lying on the copper would suffer his fury.

The ax blade sank deep into the gunhand's skull, slicing down to the man's upper palette and exposing all its gore. Torn brain matter trailed the ax blade. Before Paul could pull the double-bit ax free, the tough with the scar swung on him. Paul didn't have time to duck, but he avoided a hit straight to his nose, taking the fist under his left eye instead.

Paul stumbled back, distancing himself, readying for his next charge. The other gunhand who was still breathing ran forward within a few feet of Paul and raised his shotgun. Paul called his bluff. He'd already heard the previous order from the cloaked men. They didn't want Paul to be shot. At least, that's what he'd been hoping.

The gunhand pulled the trigger just as Paul slammed the barrel upward. The shot had been spent in vain, hitting tree branches on the other side of the clearing, but it still sent a jarring ache through Paul's head, and his ears rang from the concussion. He didn't have the luxury of waiting until it cleared. Paul grabbed the gunhand by the throat, lifted him off his feet, and slammed him to the ground. The man grunted on impact, the wind knocked out of him.

When Paul looked up, the cloaked man had once again raised the dagger over Awan's motionless body.

Before he could do anything about it, he had to face the mean bastard standing between him and the copper boulder. Paul stretched his aching neck to either side, flexed his fingers, and readied his fists. Silver Jack looked like a puppy compared to this man.

"I've heard a lot about you, Paul BonJean." The tough tipped his head as if in respect, then smirked and spit in Paul's direction.

"Have you heard that I will crush your soft skull with my bare hands?"

"Nah. I heard that you like to fight furniture and court women far above your station. I'm Samson. I'm sure my reputation precedes me."

"I have never heard of you, unless you are the ancient Samson."

"You lie, French bastard."

Paul shrugged. "Why do you talk so much? Are your hands too soft for fighting?"

Samson's smirk turned to a sneer, growling his anger at the insult, and Paul was delighted he'd taken the bait. There was nothing worse ahead of a brawl for a man to let his emotions override his senses. If that happened, he made mistakes.

Fatal mistakes.

"*Je suis prêt!*" Paul said.

Samson's face twisted in confusion, clearly not understanding Paul's declaration that he was ready.

Paul accepted the advantage, leaping toward Samson before the man could figure out what he meant. His right fist met the scarred cheek, snapping the man's head back. But the tough was fast, and he had sent a last-minute hook barreling into Paul's ribcage. Neither man could defend against the blows, and they both staggered back to an arm's length distance. The split was brief, and Paul was the first to rush forward, aiming his fist for Samson's chin.

Samson threw his left shoulder forward to catch the hit, then cracked a right to Paul's cheek. This time, they didn't break. Paul tipped his chin in and pummeled Samson's body with both fists. Scar-face held his arms up and tight to his body, keeping his chin down to protect his face behind his fists.

Merde. Samson was clearly a trained fighter. Paul didn't like the feeling that if they'd been fighting in Hell's Half Mile, his odds would have dropped dramatically.

Samson broke his guard to hit Paul with a left jab, quickly followed by a devastating uppercut that knocked the wind out of Paul. He doubled over and took Samson's knee to the face, which sent him sprawling onto his back. Paul wheezed, muscles reeling with pain, then his body tightened again as an arm snaked around his neck.

The big man pulled upward under Paul's chin, immediately cutting off his airway, and dragged him across the soft, spongy moss. Paul desperately dug his fingers between his own neck and Samson's arm until he could twist his wrist and create a break in the hold. His hands shot up to grab the forward-leaning Samson by his collar, yanking him off balance so he crashed head-first into the ground.

The moss muffled a pained grunt when Samson hit it with his face, then he fell sideways, stunned by what Paul hoped was a neck injury. Paul could barely see straight, but he could make out his ax still sticking handle-up out of a man's skull. Just as he reached for it, someone cocked a revolver and pressed a cold metal barrel against his temple.

To the Bottom

The smaller gunhand that Paul knocked the wind out of earlier was standing wide, his arm outstretched as he pressed his revolver against Paul's head. "Ah! Don't you dare do it, you French bastard."

Paul froze, eyeing the ax handle and weighing his options. It took less than a second to trigger the explosion of gunpowder in those little metal cartridges that would propel the single bullet to end him.

"No guns," a man shouted, and it wasn't Samson. The voice was a lighter tenor, and it sounded almost familiar. Then again, the locals' accents made them all sound about the same to Paul.

"Damn your rituals. If we don't kill him now. He'll—"

Samson walked up behind the young man and with one arm, swept up his gun hand and held him tight. The gun didn't discharge, even after the gunhand dropped it, and Paul felt himself sweat in relief. Samson's other hand appeared with a blade and drew it across the gunhand's throat.

Paul watched the blood gush in pulsing spurts, frozen in horror at the betrayal in Samson killing one of his own. The gunhand's mouth twitched as if he were trying to speak, but Samson had cut too deeply, severing the man's vocal cords and his trachea. His limp body fell face-first at the edge of the stream.

Samson's gaze switched to Paul.

"You ain't hard, BonJean." An inch of the knife not covered in blood gleamed, reflecting the light of the moon as it rose over the clearing. "You want the woman and the boy? Go to 'em right now."

Paul was tempted, and he couldn't deny it. If he could go straight to Awan and Thomas and save them... but it wouldn't be that easy. It *couldn't* be that easy.

There was a mean smirk painted on Samson's face, one that told Paul if he ran now to the boulder, he wouldn't be saving anyone tonight. But he nodded at the man, then swallowed hard.

Paul turned as if to go to the copper boulder, then spun back and lunged for his ax. He gripped the handle, and time seemed to slow as he somersaulted forward, barely dislodging it from the gunhand's skull as he rolled. Springing up out of the somersault, Paul judged Samson's position, then flung the ax sideways at him.

Paul watched the ax spin toward Samson in slow motion. The tough tried to dodge, his expression warping from nasty smirk to pale and horror-struck when the sharp, glinting edge of the blade sliced through his left hip, nearly cutting him in two.

Samson gasped, stumbled forward, then sprawled toward Paul. The ax had landed somewhere behind Samson, and Paul wasn't ready when Samson charged, limping toward him, fueled purely by adrenaline. He grabbed Paul by the throat with both hands, and they went over backward into the water. Tangled together, they dug fingernails into each other's flesh as they fought beneath the surface of the ice-cold water.

They sank, inch by inch. Paul never closed his eyes, watching his enemy as he used every ounce of his spirit and physical strength to overcome the tough. Each man clenched his fingers around the other's throat as they sank to the bottom of the shallow, clear stream. As his vision dimmed, Paul couldn't help but notice the shimmering image of the moon reflecting down to him through the flowing water.

Everything grew dark then, even the moon, and Paul willed himself to pull away from Samson's fingers. This couldn't be it.

He couldn't fail Thomas, Awan, and Ruby.

With the last of his energy, as his consciousness faded, Paul pulled up his feet and kicked Samson. The tough's fingers released their hold on Paul's throat, hard eyes reflecting the moonlight as he sank down to the bottom and Paul floated slowly up to the surface.

Paul broke the surface and splashed, grasping at the bank for anything to hold on to. His fingers tangled in the moss and he held on for dear life, too tired to pull himself out of the water. He choked up the water he'd swallowed and hacked, racking his lungs to get it all out.

His body shuddered as he clung to the bank, willing himself to stay afloat in the water he could have sworn wasn't as deep as it now felt. As soon as he felt he wouldn't die, the woman and the boy who needed him snapped to the forefront of his mind. He grimaced through the pain as he clawed at the bank, kicking his body onto the clearing floor. But he noticed moccasin-clad feet in his path and looked up.

There they were. The faces that had haunted him since he'd first come to the clearing. The native man who'd pushed him under the day before, and the void-filled eyes of the men and women who surrounded the edges of the clearing.

The man standing over him stared at him with those blank, black pits for eyes, no breath expanding in his chest. His hand moved slowly, fist clenching, before extending a single finger and pointing back toward the water.

"No," Paul begged, shaking his head. "I must save them!"

The man didn't move, standing still as a statue, and pointing toward where Paul had emerged from the water.

Paul tried to look past the man, but the faces all closed in on him, their bodies rushing forward, mouths stretched open too wide to be natural and filled with depthless shadow. He scrambled backward in fear as they raced toward him, falling into the water again before he could stop himself. The native man nodded slowly, then kneeled at the edge of the bank, grabbed Paul by the hair and pushed him under.

We Offer Blood

PAUL NO LONGER HAD the energy to fight, so he sank when the man pushed him under. His hand cut through the surface as he pushed Paul down, then released as Paul continued to sink. Paul watched the rhythmically waving image of the native man reflected through the water, that brilliant full moon perched just over his shoulder.

This wasn't how it was supposed to end. He'd fought like hell, killed all those men, and even defeated Samson. All of that blood and death, only to fail Awan and Thomas anyway.

Turning slowly in the water as he sank, Paul surrendered to his fate, though he still held his breath. He wouldn't simply suck in the water and become one with it just yet. Maybe that was the most stubborn part of himself, still holding on when all hope had already been extinguished. Even his eyes were still open, searching for the sandy bottom as gravity pulled him downward.

But Paul didn't see sand and rocks at the bottom of the creek. He saw light. The pulsing, watery image of a full moon. It piqued his interest, and he quickly traded mortal surrender for momentary curiosity.

Paul swam down, increasing the speed at which he sank, suddenly anxious to find the source of the moonlight at the bottom of the creek. Was it broken glass, perhaps? His arms pushed outward and his legs kicked, propelling him toward the increasingly glaring moonlight that taunted him, always just beyond his reach. He fought to swim farther down, his body fighting him to float up instead of fall downward, so he expelled the last of his breath for a final push toward the source of the moonlight.

It seemed just within reach, his eyes bulging and lungs burning as he spent the last of himself grasping at the moon.

His hand burst into the air, though he was too weak to force his body to follow it.

Something pulled at him, yanking him farther toward the bottom of the creek. His mind couldn't make sense of it, but he let the force pull him until suddenly he was out of the water and lying face-down on a mossy bank. Three fast, hard hits landed on his back, and he half-coughed, half-vomited water from his lungs and stomach until he lay exhausted, breath rasping into the pillowy forest floor.

Rough hands dragged him by his shirt for a short while, then lifted him up and dropped him on his back on something hard.

When Paul opened his weary eyes again, he was face up, staring at that bright full moon casting the gift of its light onto the darkened earth. He couldn't think straight, couldn't remember where he'd been or why. Until the chanting began again.

They started in the unfamiliar language, then again in Latin.

Realization struck him like a hammer to the gut, and he jolted upward only to find he'd been restrained. Both wrists were tied, the ropes disappearing beyond the edges of the copper boulder. Paul froze when a familiar voice broke through and halted the chanting.

"No, no. I've seen what comes when ya all finish this chant of yers, and I'm not waiting for whatever yer callin'. You pay me now, or I'll blow everybody's damn heads off before you can finish your little ritual."

Grumbled whispers, then that familiar voice again. "You hardly did the job, Jack."

"Well, he's fucking here, ain't he?"

"This matter of payment will wait until the ritual is completed!" the man argued, his voice deepening with a commanding tone.

"Just pay him so we can finish!" another man snapped urgently, sapping the leader's authority at the moment.

"Fine, damn it. Give me the saddlebags, and I'll pay you, but we're not done. Meet me back at my office, you hear?"

"Yeah, boss. Whatever yer majesty commands," Jack said, his voice dripping with sarcasm.

Paul tilted his head up and watched as one of the cloaked men passed a handful of folded bills to Silver Jack before shooing him away.

"And for you, your godforsaken saddlebags." Jack tossed the red saddlebags that had been on Bébé's saddle onto Paul's chest.

The cloaked man who'd paid Jack shot a hand forward to grab the saddlebags. He gently stroked blood-soaked leather, then gingerly placed them at Paul's feet. "You're lucky these came to no harm, Jack."

"Yeah, yeah. All right now," Jack muttered excitedly as he flipped through the bills and counted them. "I only wanted what was promised."

The chanting started again, in the unfamiliar language, but Paul, utterly speechless, could only stare at Jack. His gut hurt, but whether it was more from the physical attacks he'd endured or Jack's betrayal, he couldn't tell.

Once Jack had finished counting the money, he stuffed it in the satchel slung across his body and then tied it closed. When he looked up again, his gaze met Paul's, and he froze for a split second. Then the Irish bastard grinned and winked.

Paul felt red-hot anger swell up from his core through the top of his ears and his head until he felt like he was going to burst into flames. He strained at the ropes, his tired muscles finding new strength in the fire of his mortal fury.

The three cloaked men now chanted in Latin, though Paul barely registered it over the blood throbbing in his ears as he pulled against his bonds akin to Prometheus in the stories his father had told him.

"We offer blood to the old gods, the gods of shadow and light, that they let us harvest the bounty of the forest." The leader of the cloaked men raised the dagger high above his head, falling silent, though his companions continued chanting in Latin in fervent whispers. Moonlight reflected on the dagger's blade as it hovered above Paul, two pale hands clutching the hilt. "Ancient gods of this land, accept this offering of father, mother, and child so that the cycle may continue."

It was the final push Paul needed, and his right arm broke free just as the dagger plunged toward his heart.

But First, Monsieur...

THE RAZOR-SHARP DAGGER SLICED through the heel of Paul's palm, but his fingers gripped both of the cloaked leader's hands and squeezed, stopping the blade's deadly path. Paul fought to keep control. The man's hood had fallen back with the sudden halt of his hands and moonlight revealed a pale face and gray, scraggly hair combed across a balding spot.

"Monsieur Langley?" Paul asked, his voice barely above a whisper.

Fred Langley stared back at him, slack-jawed and speechless, his bright blue eyes wide with shock.

Paul twisted both of Fred's hands with his hand and wrenched the blade from his grasp. Langley fell forward as he lost the dagger, and Paul slammed the bottom of the hilt into his nose. The strike sent him sprawling backward, blood spraying from him. Paul sliced through the rope holding his left wrist, hacking himself free. He bolted upright, wincing against the throbbing aches over every inch of his body, and cut his legs free.

Jumping up, he held the light dagger easily in his hand, ready to slice or stab anyone who came within reach. He especially wanted a private dance with Langley. The man stood several feet back, pressing the fingers of one hand across the bridge of his nose, trying to stop the bleeding.

"Jack!" Langley shouted.

"Paul," the Irishman said from behind him.

Paul turned slowly and found both of Jack's Colts glinting in the mingled moonlight and torchlight. Jack was aiming one muzzle at Awan's motionless head and the other at Thomas's.

His chest heaving, Paul glared at Silver Jack, wishing men could be killed with a look alone, and weighed his options.

Before he could ready the dagger to hurl between Jack's eyes, the Irishman tipped the muzzles of his guns over the heads of the unconscious pair and fired two shots in quick succession.

Two men cried out as their bodies dropped, thudding to the forest floor behind Paul. He whirled, finding Langley just as surprised to see the other two cloaked men lying gut shot, writhing and groaning on their backs.

"Francis? Frankie! No, no!" Langley dropped to one man, his voice high-pitched and hysterical. "This isn't supposed to happen!"

Paul glanced over his shoulder at Jack, who spun his Colts over his fingers and slid them back into their holsters. "You'll have to take care of the last one yourself. It's in my contract that I can't kill my boss."

With that, Paul flexed his fingers over the hilt of the dagger, rolled his neck, and marched toward Langley.

Fred looked up as Paul approached, but there was no fear in his tear-filled eyes, only hatred. "You goddamned Canuck. You killed him, and our sister's husband!" He gestured to the other man, who had stilled and fallen silent. "Who the hell are you to end us? To destroy all that we've built over three generations?"

"You didn't have to do any of this," Paul said softly, bereft of any empathy he might have felt before.

"You're just another damned BonJean that no one would have missed," Fred continued, his voice shaking with sobs as he held his brother tight. "No one would have mourned you. They would piss on your grave, you French son of a bitch!"

"But first, Monsieur, they will piss on yours."

Paul grabbed Fred by the thick hair at the base of his skull, reared back with his dagger in hand, and struck the man in the eye, plunging the dagger through the socket to the hilt. He held the man by the hair even after the blade was buried as far as it would go, even as the man's mouth twitched with unspoken words and his body shook in its final throes. He dropped Langley's lifeless body onto the still corpse of his brother.

He should have felt remorse, disgust, or at least sick at the sight of all the surrounding death, but Paul was utterly numb as he stared down at the still-bleeding corpses. It was as if the God of his childhood had abandoned him, forsaken him in this cursed place.

Then he remembered Jack, and turned slowly, numbly, toward the man who was damn near his equal.

"They're all right," Jack said gently, gesturing to where Awan and Thomas lay on the ground.

"Why?" It was the only thing Paul could think to ask.

"Oh, I'll tell you. I swear it. But first, ya need to cut out the hearts of Langley, his brother, and their brother-in-law. Two hearts need to go into one side of the saddlebags, and the third on the other side."

Paul shook his head. "I am done with death and blood. I cannot—"

"You used the dagger, Paul." Jack's smirk disappeared, replaced by a deadly seriousness burning in his eyes. "The beasts are coming for us. The one who holds the dagger and completes the ritual commands them."

"Wh... What do you mean?"

"We're running out of time. Ya either keep the dagger, complete the ritual, and offer them the hearts, or none of us are leaving here alive." He tipped his head to Awan and Thomas for emphasis.

"How do you know all of this?"

"Because I…" Jack swallowed hard and looked away. "I helped them last year. Before you say anything, Paul, I was down on my luck and desperate. People were looking for me in the west, and I needed the work. I needed to eat."

"What changed?"

"It won't fucking matter if you don't complete the ritual!"

As if to validate Jack's point, there was movement in the brush from the west, north, and east.

"*Câlice, d'accord!*" Paul reached down, put one boot on Langley's skull, grabbed the dagger in both hands, and wrenched it free. Then he dropped to his knees and stabbed the knife into Langley's lifeless chest repeatedly until he made a hole big enough for his hand. He plunged his left hand into the slick cavity and twisted until he ripped the heart free.

Now, as he studied the human heart held in the palm of his hand in the glow of torchlight, he felt something. Despair, he thought, for whatever chance his soul had at eternal life. Some things, things as depraved as this, surely could not be forgiven by a mere confession.

He worked the saddlebags out from under Langley's body as the movements in the brush came closer to the edge of the wood line, and it seemed to halt them momentarily. Encouraged by this—and for the sakes of Awan and Thomas—Paul made quick work of the other two and did as Jack had instructed.

"Bring the saddlebags here," Jack said, patting a hand on the boulder. Paul froze upon seeing the boulder clear of bodies until Jack waved at where he'd laid the woman and the boy near the horses. "They'll be fine if we finish this."

The first creature to cross the wood line into the clearing was the giant, scarred bear that had chased Paul, Makwa, and Jack the day before. Paul found it odd that so little time had passed. Yesterday felt like a lifetime ago.

The bear sat on its haunches and watched him hungrily.

Paul raised the dagger in his right hand and set the bloody saddlebags of human hearts on the massive copper boulder. Another creature stepped into the clearing; it appeared to be a wolf, though it was larger than any he'd ever seen. Strangest of all, the creature stood on its hind legs. The eyes that met his were eerily human-like.

The brush rustled and moved again, and a third creature entered the clearing. Antlers sprouted from its mangy, narrow skull; its skin pulled tight across the bones. The deer-like head glared back at him with sickly, ruby-colored orbs set deep in its eye sockets, though the rest of its body was nearly human—at least if humans could grow to eight feet tall. And then the chill-inducing realization struck Paul: this was the creature he'd seen in '65, the one Viggo had saved him from.

"Please tell me ya can repeat those words in Latin that Langley and his boys chanted."

"I *must* repeat those words?"

"I can't say what will happen if we don't. But I know the two of us can't take them all."

"Agreed," Paul said as he studied the creatures. He recalled the words the men had chanted and urged his tongue to remember how to make the sounds he'd used in the Latin prayers drilled into his brain as a child.

"Sanguinem diis antiquis offerimus, diis umbrae et lucis, ut nobis permittant segetem silvae metere. Diis antiquis huius terrae, hoc sacrificium accipite, ut cursus vitae continuet."

The scarred bear, the walking wolf, and the decaying, fanged deer creature all crouched and snarled at him.

A Single Heart

Paul waited for the moment the bizarre creatures would launch at him and Jack. He flexed the fingers of his left hand, ready to fight one last time, even if he couldn't win. Jack stood stock-still, watching the creatures snarl and roar.

Paul still held the dagger, though he was sure the single blade wouldn't do much to the three mountains of flesh, bones, teeth, and claws.

"Offer the hearts," Jack whispered.

Using the dagger, Paul slipped the blade under the center of the saddlebags and lifted them to the edge of the copper boulder. He knew the metal must be important, just as the boulders in the other two clearings had been important. He stepped backward and lowered the dagger to his side, and Jack mirrored his movement.

The first to come forward was the deer-skulled creature. Paul couldn't tell if it was actually staring at him, but he had the sense that the hungry eyes of a predator studied him. It was the same sensation he had felt the night he and Awan had watched the darkness. And then, silhouetted by moonlight as it stepped toward the copper boulder, Paul recognized the antlers. They were the very antlers he'd seen the night Thomas had sworn he saw something staring at them from the darkness.

Whatever this creature was from all those years ago and only nights before, it had been stalking them. It had known they were coming. It had waited for them.

An elongated, clawed hand reached into one side of the saddlebags and pulled out a single heart. The creature raised the dead muscle to its fanged mouth and bit into it. Sharp fangs sliced into the tough flesh, then jerked sideways to tear out a chunk. Blood squirted from the heart and dripped down the creature's strange maw, but it seemed satisfied. It kept the heart in one hand, working its jaw to chew the piece it had torn off as it backed out of the clearing. Its body disappeared beyond the torchlight, and for a few seconds, the only thing Paul could see were its ruby-red orbs still tracking him.

Paul fought the shiver that threatened to shake him. There were still two more of the old gods to satisfy.

The standing wolf was the next to accept the offering, silent as the last, when its paw morphed into a human hand and slipped one of the hearts from the saddlebags. Its bright gold eyes seemed to bore through his soul as it opened its mouth and sank its glistening fangs into the second heart. Something popped in the heart as the teeth crunched into it, and blood sprayed over the copper. The spray landed near where the first creature had dripped some on the boulder, and Paul knew without complete understanding that it was important that the blood of the heart spilled on the copper.

Satisfied, the wolf clenched the rest of the heart in his teeth. His hand transformed back into a giant gray paw, and he dropped to all fours before trotting off into the darkness beyond the wood line.

Last to take the offering was the scarred bear with its gleaming red eyes. Paul opened the flap of the saddlebag with the dagger and positioned the opening toward the bear. The bear chuffed, rocking on its feet as it stared him down, tossing the occasional glance at

Jack. Finally, it rose on its hind legs and approached as the other two creatures had.

"Look," Jack whispered as it approached, gesturing inconspicuously toward a spot behind the bear.

Paul dared a look and felt understanding dawn on him.

Behind the giant scarred bear waited two red-eyed cubs, sitting on their haunches and silently watching their mother.

The mother bear approached the copper boulder, stuck her talons in the open saddlebag, and fished out the final heart. As any bear would with fish or flesh, she held the heart in both paws, dropped on her haunches, and chewed it greedily. More drops of blood in a spot next to the blood spray of the heart bitten by the gray wolf. Gnawing, tearing, squelching sounds threatened to twist Paul's stomach, but he dared not move or make a sound.

He knew that if he hadn't gotten free to stop the dagger aimed for his chest—and certainly if Jack hadn't double-crossed Langley—it would be his own heart being eaten.

The scarred bear gave a quick grunt as it eyed both Paul and Jack, then returned to her cubs. She let out a series of grunts as she reached them, and they followed her into the shadows north of the clearing.

"The mother of the forest," a soft voice said from behind them.

Paul spun, his vision blurring when he spotted Awan standing before him. Without a moment's hesitation, he rushed forward and embraced her, lifting her off her feet. As soon as the impropriety registered in his mind, he gently set her back on the earth and stepped back, holding her hands instead. "*Je suis desolé,* Awan. I am only happy to see you are awake."

"Thanks to you," she said, smirking softly. Then she turned her gaze on Jack. "And even to you."

Jack nodded, letting his gaze fall. "I'm sorry I couldn't move sooner, but if I moved too quick, I wouldn't have been around when I was needed the most."

"Mother of the forest, you said?" Paul asked, still holding Awan's hands. He gave them a soft squeeze before letting them go. "How much did you see?"

"The first creature, the one who's been stalking us since we left Oscoda, represents hunger, starvation, lack of all things needed to sustain life. It must be fed, or it will consume all who enter its domain. The wolf? He is the father of the forest, a creature of stealth and wisdom. And the bear is the mother of the forest, its protector, huntress, and caretaker. They needed to feed the spirits of the forest to keep them from destroying the camps they set up here in this wild place."

Jack nodded. "That was the reason for all," he gestured around the clearing, "this. To appease what they called 'the old gods'. Some dark sorcery they brought from the Old World, blood rituals and human sacrifice. I... I'm sorry I didn't come clean sooner."

He listened to Awan and Jack as he checked on Thomas. The boy appeared to be sleeping on his bed of soft, spongy moss, so Paul grabbed a blanket from one of the gunhands' horses and covered him with it. Thomas's face was calm, peaceful, and his breath came slow.

"I am glad you did not wait longer." Paul sighed and met Jack's gaze. "You did right by us today, Jack. *Merci*. And what happens now?"

He returned to Awan's side near the copper boulder. He traced his fingers over the alternating rough patches and smooth spots, avoiding the drips and trickles of blood.

"They are fed. Now the company can take all they want from the land this winter, its water, its creatures, the ancient trees and all their gifts."

"Hmm. But will there be a company without the Langley brothers?"

"Who cares?" Jack shook his head, then whistled. "I don't know about you, but I'm ready to get the hell out of here."

The thundering hooves of a pair of horses came rushing toward them, and Paul's heart lifted when Bébé cantered straight over to him. She stopped near him, tossing her head and smelling him, her eyes filled with fear as she took in the scent of blood. Snorting and blowing, she sniffed the ground, then raised her head up to inspect him again.

Paul chuckled low. "I am fine, girl."

He searched for a moment and finally found his ax lying cold in the moss, and he strapped it to his saddle. Sometime much later, he'd take the time to scrub off all the blood and gore.

"Let's ride," Awan suggested, walking to Thomas and kneeling before running her slender finger over his brown hair. "Who will ride with Thomas?"

"I will," Paul answered immediately. "When he wakes, he'll have his own horse." He nodded to the extra horses still tied at the eastern edge of the clearing. "Awan, pick your horse, and Jack, set up a pony line."

"Hey, now. You ain't the boss no more."

Paul didn't bother toying with Silver Jack, instead focusing on gently lifting a wool blanket-wrapped Thomas into Bébé's saddle before climbing up himself. As he expected, both had done as he'd asked. Awan had picked a palomino morgan, and Jack was setting up all the horses on a pony line. They'd be excellent stock for keeping or selling.

Once they were ready, they strapped the lanterns to the saddles along the line of horses. Jack rode in front, leading their way out of the forest the same way they'd left this clearing before with Makwa. Only this time, thankfully, the giant bear wasn't chasing them.

Awan rode at the back with Paul, riding quietly beside him wherever the trail allowed. He couldn't help but notice her staring at him every so often. Sometimes the lantern light reflected in her intelligent, pretty eyes, and he felt like he was being watched by a predator again. Only this time, he wasn't worried about being eaten alive.

Makwa came thundering up on Kitchi, meeting them just as they left the tree line and could feel the open air of the stumpfields again. He waved to Jack, but didn't even slow until he reached the end of the line of horses. He slid to a stop and leaned in his saddle to hug his sister.

He spoke to her in their language, his voice filled with pain, worry, and relief all at once. She spoke gently but firmly, never letting him interrupt when it was her turn to speak.

"Makwa has always loved you as a brother, Paul," she said in English suddenly, ignoring the obvious protest of her little brother. "I think we should make him legally your brother."

"Huh?" Paul couldn't imagine what she meant. Were there laws in America that allowed a man to designate his own family?

"What tribe was she from?"

"Who?"

"Whatever relative gave you your dark eyes and cheekbones."

"Ah, my *grand-mére*. She was Algonquin."

Awan nodded approvingly.

"Try to be proper," Makwa pleaded, but she cut him off.

"You will marry me, Paul," she stated plainly, then smiled. "Before you leave for the winter camps."

Makwa flopped forward over Kitchi's mane and groaned dramatically.

Paul sat there staring at Awan as the horses followed the trail east at a simple walk.

There beneath the starlight and light of a full moon falling toward the horizon, he knew in his heart that she was right. She was the only woman tough enough in mind, spirit, and body who could tame a brute like him. And he'd known the spark he'd pushed down since the moment he first saw her, brushing it off as mere curiosity.

"Makwa," Paul said, poking his friend on the shoulder. "Is this okay with you?"

The man sighed, pushed himself upright, and shook his head with a grin. "You've been chosen, Paul. I couldn't tell her otherwise—even if I wanted to."

Paul smiled back at Awan and tipped his head in respect. "*Oui, mademoiselle.*"

It seemed he already had a new boss, and this one was a far sight prettier than the last.

Thomas stirred then, leaning as he was against Paul's left arm at the front of the saddle. His eyes opened slowly with grogginess, but he pushed himself to sit up.

"Makwa, tell Jack to stop so we can get Thomas his own horse."

Makwa, still looking mortified, trotted off to the front and called out to Jack.

"Where are we?" the boy asked.

"We are on the way home. Do not worry. You will be with your aunt Ruby soon."

Thomas swallowed hard, shook his head, and stared up at Paul with fear in his eyes.

My Loyalty and My Silence

PAUL HELPED THE BOY onto the jet-black shire gelding Jack had brought for him. "You can speak freely. We've gone through so much to make sure you are safe."

They had stopped all the horses so Thomas could get his own mount, and now Jack pulled up close to the rest of them, his eyes hard as he listened in.

"We will keep you safe, Thomas," Awan added, resting a gentle hand on the boy's shoulder.

He stared down at her from the back of his much taller horse, and the tears fell. "She's not my aunt."

"What?!" Paul asked, so stunned he halted Bébé.

Thomas shook his head. "I've been on the streets with my big sister since our parents passed." He sniffled a little and wiped his tears with the back of one hand. "They took Sarah and said if I didn't help you, they'd make her do... she'd have to do what the women do."

"How old is your sister?" Awan shot a worried look at Paul before focusing on the boy again.

"Eleven."

"*Mon Dieu!*" Paul shook his head, tightening his grip on the reins.

"Paul," Jack started. "I took Langley to Hell's Half Mile just before we left. To the Red Bird Saloon. He met the owner, Matthew Smith, and Ruby was with him."

"The father, the mother, and the child," Paul mumbled, glancing between Awan and Thomas. Langley wanted a child to sacrifice. And Ruby had played Paul like a fiddle. She'd known exactly how to get a child on the expedition without Paul suspecting anything.

"Where is your sister now, Thomas?"

"They have her," the boy said, his voice small and shaking. "Please don't let them hurt her, Mister Paul."

"He won't let them hurt her," Awan said, then her eyes flashed to Paul. "Isn't that right?"

Paul couldn't hold back a proud grin as he gazed back at her. Every pain and ache seemed to disappear as he basked in the glow of her expectation and faith. "That is right."

"Let's handle this final matter, Paul," Jack said, tipping his head toward the trail before them.

Paul nodded. "Makwa, get them to safety with the others and camp out for two days. One of us will come to get you when it's safe."

"I can do that," his future brother-in-law agreed.

"Promise you'll return." Awan stared at him, pressing, but her eyes showed no fear.

"Of course. And," he glanced at Thomas, then back at her, "how do you feel about starting our family with two children?"

She smiled broadly in approval. "I expect nothing less."

Paul gave her a wink, then turned his horse and spurred her into a gallop.

Jack followed, and as the trail opened up, they rode side by side until they came to a split. Both horses slid to a stop and heaved for breath while the two men considered the path forward.

"East goes to Oscoda," Paul said.

"And south to Bay City."

"It's a long ride, but the ferry won't be here for hours."

"Let them catch their breath," Jack gestured to the horses, "and we'll figure out a plan."

"And you can explain why you betrayed Langley." Paul tapped his fingers against the still-bloody ax blade as they veered their horses south along the trail at a walk. "Why should I trust you?"

Jack eyed the ax, then returned his gaze to the trail ahead, his expression growing somber. "Anyone who's heard me speak for more than a word or two can tell I'm Irish."

Paul nodded, not taking his eyes off the man.

"Well, this Langley character hired me last year, and hardly said two words to me the entire trip. Always looking down at me, he was. But that's nothing new. Most people do that. And like I said before, I didn't like the work, but I needed the money, and he bought my loyalty and my silence."

That was something Paul understood. Companies were only loyal as far as they needed a man, and so men were only loyal as far as they needed a company. What Jack had with Langley was a business arrangement.

"This year, when we're setting all this bloody mess up for you and the crew, he prattles on to me about his English heritage all high and mighty like. He keeps runnin' his mouth, talking about how he comes from some noble family or somethin'. I fuckin' hate the English, but the man's paying me, so I keep my mouth shut.

"But then this limey bastard spouts off something about potatoes and dirty Irish peasants, and I was seeing red, BonJean." Jack shook his head fervently. "I wanted to strangle him right there in front of his mousey little clerk and all them people coming in for their pay. More than anything, I wanted to watch the light leave his eyes."

Red-faced, Jack grumbled at the memory, and Paul could feel the anger rolling off him.

"This happened after our brawl, and so I thought, why am I siding with this bag of shit over a real man who's got some fight in 'im? Ya don't hire no one to do yer dirty work; yer the one who gets his hands dirty and still holds his head high."

Paul nodded. "We had a fight from hell."

"Ya best believe we did. So I decided then and there that I'd kill Langley before he could kill ya."

"Then why didn't you shoot him before he tried to knife me?!"

Jack rubbed the back of his neck. "As I said, Paul, it was written plainly in my contract. I could hurt whoever I needed to get the job done, but I couldn't be the one to bring harm to Langley."

Scoffing, Paul shook his head, unsatisfied.

"Ya don't think I have honor? Let me explain somethin' to ya. I came here from Ireland in '60, Paul. Barely here, two years before, my cousins convinced me to join the Irish Brigade when the country split. I fought at Antietam."

Paul understood suddenly, and he watched the muscles in Jack's face tense.

"I fought at Bloody Lane, and somehow, some way, I survived. God, I wish I had a drink." He slowly dropped the reins over the horn of his saddle and pointed to his Colts. "They're both Army Colts. One that was issued to me, and one issued to the only brother I had left until that awful day. And that, Pauly, is why I carry two Army Colts. I keep 'em clean, and I never forget that for some damned reason, the Almighty saw fit for my brother to die that day instead of me."

"I am sorry, Jack."

"He was a good man, a better man than I could ever be. Some days, I hold his gun, and I feel like tryin' to be a bit more like him. Today, my brother was with me, and he fought for ya, too."

Paul reached out a hand and clapped it on Jack's shoulder. "When you say your prayers tonight, send your brother thanks from me."

Jack said nothing in the pre-dawn air, and they rode in silence for the rest of the morning, alternating their speed between a hard gallop and walking to rest the horses.

Now that he understood Silver Jack a little better and had his answers, Paul was ready to trust him. They rode hard, arriving in Bay City just after dark and leaving their horses at the livery for care. And then they marched, Paul carrying his ax at his side, trying to be as natural as possible, and Silver Jack with his Colts slung low under his jacket.

One for Me, and One for You

WHEN THEY ENTERED THE Red Bird, the place was empty except for the bartender reading a paper behind the bar. He looked up over a pair of delicate spectacles. "We're closed tonight."

"I'm here to deliver a message from Langley," Silver Jack said, stopping just inside the doorway with Paul at his side. "It's important."

The bartender hesitated and glanced at Paul.

"He's with me."

"I don't know. Mr. Smith was very particular in his instructions."

In a flash, Silver Jack had one of the Colts out of his holster and aimed at the man, who jumped back, holding his hands up.

"P-please," he begged in a half-whisper.

Jack walked behind the bar, keeping his gun trained on the bartender all the while, and grabbed the man by the collar before slowly dragging him out into the open.

"Either ya get out and pretend ya were never here, never seen us, or I'm going to let the BonJean treat you like he treats the pines."

The man shuddered, and half-ducked as if Paul was already coming with his ax. "I n-never saw you!"

"There now. See? Good man. And if you forget you didn't see us, there's no man of God or the law that can save you from me. Do you hear?"

He nodded, teeth clenched and raised hands trembling.

"Go out the back," Paul said, keeping his voice low.

Jack walked the man toward the rear of the building, disappearing down a darkened hallway and returning a few seconds later. "That one will never breathe a word of this. We have time."

They locked the front door of the saloon and headed up to Smith's office. None of the other girls were present, even though they lived here. All was still, all was quiet as they slowly, gently climbed the stairs. As they approached the door to Smith's office, they could hear the chanting.

The same Latin words Paul had recognized from the forest, and a fire switched on instantly within him. His skin grew hot, and his vision tinted red as if his eyes were covered in fresh, warm blood.

"Are you alright, Paul?" Jack whispered next to Paul's head, but his voice sounded far away.

"No. We... have to... stop them."

"Let's go then." Jack drew his pistols from their holsters and kicked the wooden door open.

The door splintered, shards of the thin material spinning away, and Paul could barely contain himself when he saw what was happening.

A girl that could have been a twin to Thomas was tied at the wrists and ankles, lashed to furniture that held her arms above her head as she lay in the middle of the floor. They had dressed her in something that must have been one of Ruby's older gowns, clearly out of fashion now.

Smith turned as soon as they entered, anger scrawled through the deep lines on his weathered, mean face. He held high a dagger matching the one Paul now carried, and it was aimed over the girl's chest. Ruby stared up at Paul, her face frozen in shock as she held forward a copper bowl that he suspected was meant to collect the poor girl's heart.

"You scream, I shoot," Jack explained quickly. "You move wrong, I shoot. If ya even breathe in a way I don't like, I'll be decorating the walls with your brains. Do we have an understanding?"

Smith nodded, unmoving.

"I'll be taking that," Jack said, holstering his right pistol so he could take the dagger in his dominant hand. He cut the girl free while Paul held his ax in both hands, ready to swing on Smith or Ruby if either moved. "Sarah?"

She nodded, then asked in a hoarse voice through her tears, "Have you seen my brother?"

"Thomas is safe with our people," Paul explained, resisting the temptation to go berserk with his ax. "And we have promised to take you and your brother in as our own. If that is what you want, of course."

It was getting hard to breathe. He only had to hold back a little longer.

She nodded, tears streaming down her cheeks.

"Do you know where St. Mary's is? Go there and wait for Awan."

"And do us a favor, will you? When you head downstairs, go out the back door."

"Thank you," Sarah said through quivering lips. She wiped her tears as she fled out of the room and down the stairs.

"Monsieur," Ruby started, her voice thick like honey and soft as silk.

Paul ignored her, waiting until he heard a door shut downstairs before he spoke again. "Ready, Jack?"

"What should we do with these two?"

"It looks like they need a heart to offer," Paul observed, his voice not sounding his own as he surrendered to the bloodlust building within him. "I think they need two. One for me, and one for you."

Jack chuckled, his voice vibrating low through the room. "I believe I catch your meaning. You get to work on that little siren, and I'll handle this worm."

They bathed the room in blood, brains, and intestines, reveling in the destruction of flesh. After they'd cut their enemies open, Paul and Jack surrendered to the call of the old gods and finished the ritual they'd begun in the forest. They devoured the hearts of Ruby and Matthew Smith, satiating the awakened beasts within them. Before dawn, they too left by the back door.

Twisted Tales of Familiar Faces

If you enjoyed this bone-chilling retelling of the *Paul Bunyan* legend, don't miss out on the rest of this horrifying collection!

Humbug (Scrooge) - Andre Gonzalez

Sweethaven (Popeye) - RJ Clark

Timber Beast (Paul Bunyan) - A.K. Hughey

Alice (Alice in Wonderland) - Audrey Brice

Wish (Aladdin) - Courtney Konstantin

Quixote (Don Quixote) - Stephen Wertzbaugher

Arturius (King Arthur) - A.K. Hughey

Steamboat (Steamboat Willie) - Courtney Konstantin

Strangled (Rapunzel) - Stephen Wertzbaugher

Dethroning Oz (Wizard of Oz) - Audrey Brice

Scorned (Hercules) - Z.S. Diamanti

Check out the entire collection at www.m4lpublishing.com

Join our newsletter to stay up to date with all upcoming releases at www.m4lpublishing.com

Author's Note

To my parents, thank you for sharing in the adventure of exploring Michigan's northeastern lumber country with me and my children. Your enthusiasm and curiosity brought the stories of the forests to life.

To my children, who make every trip "up north" unforgettable—thank you for turning our days of camping, playing in the lakes and rivers, and wandering through the old-growth forests at Hartwick Pines into cherished memories.

To my husband for encouraging my pursuit of history to inform my narrative, and for always supporting my creative endeavors.

To Niki and Courtney, your encouragement came at just the right moments, lifting me up when doubt tried to pull me down.

And to Nan, for being both an incredible editor and a relentless champion of my work—thank you for pushing me to keep writing, even when the trail ahead seemed uncertain.

Enjoy this book?

We hope you enjoyed this release from M4L Publishing.

Reviews are the most helpful tools in getting new readers for any books. We don't have the financial backing of a New York publishing house and can't afford to blast our books on billboards or bus stops.

(Not yet!)

That said, your honest review can go a long way in helping us reach new readers. If you've enjoyed this book, we'd be forever grateful if you could spend a couple minutes leaving it a review (it can be as short as you like) on the site you purchased this book from.

Thank you so much!

About the author

A.K. Hughey invokes her B.A. in English and M.A. in Ancient and Classical History to craft chilling horror tales steeped in culture and dripping with lore. Specializing in paranormal and historical horror, along with vigilante thrillers, she weaves stories that captivate and terrify. Residing in the cryptid-filled heart of Appalachia, A.K. stalks the eerie landscape for inspiration and shares her home with her family and her feline overlords.